KNIGHTS OF THE HILL COUNTRY

WITHDRAWN

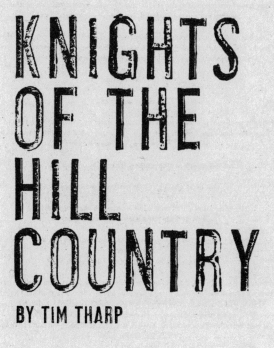

KNIGHTS OF THE HILL COUNTRY

BY TIM THARP

Published by Laurel-Leaf
an imprint of Random House Children's Books
a division of Random House, Inc.
New York

This is a work of fiction. Names, characters, places, and incidents either are the
product of the author's imagination or are used fictitiously. Any resemblance to
actual persons, living or dead, events, or locales is entirely coincidental.

Originally published in hardcover in the United States by Alfred A. Knopf Books for
Young Readers, New York, in 2006. This edition published by arrangement with
Alfred A. Knopf Books for Young Readers.

Laurel-Leaf and colophon are registered trademarks of Random House, Inc.

Visit us on the Web! www.randomhouse.com/teens

Educators and librarians, for a variety of teaching tools,
visit us at www.randomhouse.com/teachers

The Library of Congress has cataloged the hardcover edition of this work as follows:
Tharp, Tim.
Knights of the hill country / Tim Tharp.
p. cm.
Summary: In his senior year, high school star linebacker Hampton Green finally begins to
think for himself and discovers that he might be interested in more than just football.
ISBN: 978-0-375-83653-4 (trade) — ISBN: 978-0-375-93653-1 (lib. bdg.)
[1. Coming of age—Fiction. 2. Football—Fiction. 3. Identity—Fiction.
4. High schools—Fiction. 5. Schools—Fiction. 6. Oklahoma—Fiction.] I. Title.
PZ7.T32724Kn 2006
[Fic]—dc22
2005033279

ISBN: 978-0-553-49513-3 (pbk.)

RL: 5.8
Reprinted by arrangement with Alfred A. Knopf Books for Young Readers
August 2008
Printed in the United States of America
10 9 8 7 6 5 4 3
First Laurel-Leaf Edition

MANY THANKS TO: my agent, Emily Sylvan Kim, and my editor, Michele Burke; everyone at Knopf who worked on this book; Nick, Katie, Clint, Charlene, and Bill for long-term support; literary consultants Paden, Abby, Cindy, and David Treadway; and advisors Keith Hunter, James Aquino, Cynthia Weiner, Stacey Richter, Maryellen Linnehan, Brad Hughes, John Cooper (for last time), and Dennis Huggins, former coach of the Class 6A state football champions, the Midwest City Bombers.

CHAPTER ONE

I done it. I stopped time.

Every single player on that football field locked up stiff as them wax figures they got over in the Pawtuska Wild West Wax Museum. Made quite a picture, the stadium lights blazing overhead like fractured stars and the football froze slick and hard as a rocket against the night sky, our outside linebacker's fingers stretching just an inch too short to do a thing but let it fly over. I had to admit it was a thing of pure beauty, that pass, even if it was the enemy quarterback that thrown it. Tight spiral. Perfect arc. That boy had talent. But, sorry to say, it wasn't going to be enough. Not with me freezing time like I could.

Course, time didn't really stop. I didn't wave no magic wand or poof out a cloud of fairy dust or crank up some science-fiction machine with spinning gears and flashing lights on it. Thing was, I'd focus so hard that I'd squinch everything down so it *seemed* like time froze just long enough for me to look and see what I'd have to do next. That was my talent, the one and only thing I knew how to do better than anyone else around.

I had me this math teacher one time back in junior high, Mr. Moon, told me it was too bad they'd passed them child labor laws 'cause I'd do a lot more good hauling coal up out of a mine twelve hours a day than I done wasting desk space in his classroom. Big, redheaded dumb jock, that's all he seen, and he wasn't the only one probably neither. But none of them folks knew what went on in my head. Not one had the least idea who the real me was.

The scene whirled back up to full speed, and over by the sideline, the ball snapped right into the Wynette receiver's hands. Our little old Vietnamese cornerback, Tommy Nguyen, grabbed at the receiver's jersey, but he couldn't get ahold of it firm and spilled off to the side. Poor Tommy. That was bound to earn him a good chunk of grief at practice on Monday. After that, number eighty-eight tucked the ball under his arm, juked, and zigzagged into the open. Had him twenty-five yards of open pasture clean to the end zone, and I knew he was thinking surefire touchdown. He was thinking, *I'm the hero now, buddy boy. Nothing left but to figure out which way I'm gonna spike the ball and dance around the goalpost.*

One problem. Old eighty-eight had no way of guessing I'd done predicted every one of them moves before he even seen he was going to make them his own bad self. I aimed at just the right angle to cut him off and charted my route so perfect, all your math geniuses with every protractor and compass in the world couldn't have mapped it out better. His reputation as an all-state sprinter didn't make an ounce of difference and neither did the fact that he'd scored him something like a sixty-yard touchdown in the game before this one. I had me the perfect angle and just enough speed so that at the exact right moment, I launched through the air, a high-powered torpedo straight on target, and—*bam!*—I slammed into him broadside, both of us crashing hard into the ground, dirt flying up in my face and chalk dust stinging my nostrils.

Getting up to my feet, I had just about every teammate of mine on the sideline slapping my back, telling me, "Good tackle. Attaboy, Hamp, you killed that sucker—attaboy, attaboy, Hamp." The stands flat-out boomed with cheers. But eighty-eight, he was still laying on his back, this kind of stunned look glazing over his eyes behind his face mask. He looked about like a lost little first grader down there. I couldn't help but feel sorry for him. He come so close to being the hero. It was like he'd tried on a new outfit and seen how good it looked and everything, and then someone come along and told him he had to put it back on the rack. Poor guy. I reached my hand down and he took it, and after helping him pull hisself up, I slapped him on the butt and sent him back off across the field.

Big mistake.

"Hampton!" It was my buddy Blaine Keller barking at me. He strictly plays offense, so he had his helmet off and his black hair was pasted to his forehead, the black slashes of war paint under his eyes starting to run some from the sweat. "Don't give your hand to the enemy like that. This is a battle, son. Don't ever give your hand to the enemy during a battle."

He meant business too. You could tell by the way the

3

sparks flared up in his brown eyes. He wasn't faking. He was mad. I jogged back to the defensive huddle, feeling like I'd had the air half let out of me. Tell you what, Coach Huff and his assistants was some of the best coaches in Oklahoma—and I figured you might as well throw Texas in there too. Everything about them was polished and sharp as a new pair of scissors—their clothes, their hair, and their orders most of all. But they was always distant, up on another level looking down. Blaine was my best friend, my brother almost, and his words cut deeper than anyone else's.

He was right, I thought. That always was my shortcoming right there. Too much sympathy. It was like Blaine used to tell me, "Feeling sorry for folks never won no football games."

This wasn't any time to go weak neither. This was a time a guy needed insides about as tough and gnarled and hard as one of them old blackjack oaks on the hills outside of town. Me and the rest of the Kennisaw Knights had us eighteen yards and twenty-seven inches of battleground to defend. Three minutes and thirty-four seconds left in the game. First and ten. Kennisaw 20 and the Wynette Titans 17.

Every game this season, the pressure weighed down more and more. It was like carrying around a sack full of rocks, only every time you got to thinking you could lay it down, someone would throw another sack full of bigger rocks up on top of you. If we could keep it going, this would be Kennisaw's fifth undefeated season in a row. For thirty-some years, no Knights team had strung together that many wins, and them old-time players from back then was still heroes around the hill country of eastern Oklahoma. More than just heroes, they was flat-out legends.

Now, people love their legends in the hill country. I don't

just mean the ones that run up and down the green fields there in Biggins Stadium with its crown of golden lights neither. I'm talking about the old-timey Wild West legends like the Doolins and the Daltons and Belle Starr, the queen of the outlaws. All them famous characters in the wax museum. And then you got your bull riders and bronc busters, your Five Civilized Tribes and your wildcat oil strikers. Pretty Boy Floyd and Woody Guthrie, Will Rogers, Mickey Mantle, and the original great football player Jim Thorpe hisself. Kennisaw's a dusty little old town, but even the smallest scrawny kid can feel big if he's got hisself a legend to hold on to.

And believe you me, not a player on our team didn't think about what kind of legends we could end up being our own selves if we finished off this fifth straight season undefeated. Boy howdy. The Kennisaw Knights was the best damn football team in all the hill country, where Friday-night high school football ranked next to God and country, and, truth be known, sometimes come in first. It'd be one hell of a big sack of rocks to carry around if you let the Knights down.

Every mouth on the Kennisaw side of the stadium let loose a roar of "Defense! Defense! Defense!" Taking my position there at middle linebacker, I could feel it rumbling through my chest and stomach, all the way out into my arms and legs. It was almost like that crowd was creating me out of thin air right on the spot. Outside the stands, the rest of the town would be as bare as a soup bone 'cause everyone was right here at the game, chanting up their spell. Bankers and mechanics, dental hygienists, the glass-plant gang, farmers, store clerks, and doctors. Even Miss Nikomos, the dance-school teacher. Everyone.

Almost.

CHAPTER TWO

Now, if what I'm telling you about the things I done in football this season sounds like bragging, I don't mean it to. Sure, I ate them cheers up like a starving orphan with a hunk of bread, but I never thought for a second they made me better than anyone else. I probably felt more like the opposite most of the time.

Fact was, whatever I accomplished in the sport of football, I owed all to Blaine Keller and his dad. They was the ones that started me in it back in grade school, and they taught me the fundamentals and coached me every step of the way and even tried to hammer the right attitude into me, though I guess that part never did take too good.

If it hadn't been for Blaine and football, who knows what would've become of me. Lord knows, I sure didn't get any looking-after at home. Probably would've ended up one of them big meaty sullen types like old Casey Guyman. Wearing the plaid shirts with the sleeves cut out and smoking cigarettes off on the outskirts of the school grounds, waiting for after-school detention to start. Walking down the railroad tracks alone 'cause everyone's scared to be friends with him. It ain't far-fetched at all to think that might've been me.

So when the fans started chanting my name like they done in that game against the Titans, I felt good, all right, but I didn't get the big head or nothing like that. I knew durn well I was lucky to get away with batting that ball down instead of having a touchdown scored on me, and Blaine didn't let me forget it neither.

After we held the Titans off on fourth down, I jogged off the field and hadn't no more than hit the sideline when Blaine started in yelling, "Hampton, get over here, dammit!" He grabbed my jersey and jerked me up next to him. "You was out of position on that pass play."

"I got adjusted all right, though," I said.

"You do something like that again, and I'll adjust your ass!" He slammed his palm against the side of my helmet and stared me down hard. The old Blaine stare. Before I could get out another word, he popped his mouthpiece into his mouth, whipped around, and jogged off for the huddle, checking out the scoreboard on his way.

I knew what he was thinking, the real thing that was eating at him. Too much time left. It was up to him and the offense to run the time out now, and that wouldn't be easy with the way Wynette was playing, biting and yapping like a pack of little terriers that thought they was bigger than they really was.

Last season, I wouldn't have worried. Last season, Blaine

was The Man. Leading rusher and leading scorer in the division. So fast and tough and quick, trying to tackle him was like running into a tornado full of barbwire. Nothing could've stopped him from banging out a first down or two, maybe even a touchdown in a game like this. Making big plays was his stock-in-trade. But that was before the thing with his knee.

It happened at the end of last season in the Okalah game. Everybody knew them Okalah Outlaws was the dirtiest players in the state, so it wouldn't surprise me none if they went after Blaine's knee on purpose. And that's what he said too. Swore he'd get even with them someday. What happened was, two of their boys hit him at the same time—the cornerback and that fat linebacker with the broken front tooth. It was the cornerback's helmet that speared him straight in the knee, but Blaine figured they was both in on the plan, a high-low hit to take him out of the game. Didn't work, though. Blaine's about as tough as an old ring-nosed rodeo bull—mean as one too when he has to be. He finished out the game, playing on nothing but guts and stubbornness, that knee burning from the inside out so bad he told me he was surprised his britches didn't catch on fire from it.

But he didn't tell nobody else and ordered me to shut up about it too. Said there wasn't nothing worth telling. You should've seen that knee, though, all swole up like a big hairy cantaloupe. He finished out the season without complaint one—Knights don't whine—and come summer he said he was as good as a brand-new Cadillac. But I knew better.

Out on the field the huddle broke, and I toed up to the sideline, yelling, "First down, boys! First down's all we need! Come on now, offense! Come on now! You can do it!"

The game plan was simple—bang it up the middle, eat up time and yardage. Blaine lined up in the I, and he did something probably nobody but me noticed. He pounded down on his right kneepad a couple times, like maybe he could wake up that stiff old knee and get the speed out of it again like he used to.

"You're the man, Blaine!" I hollered. "You're the man!"

Old Sweetpea Lewis snapped the ball off to Darnell, and Darnell wheeled around and slammed it into Blaine's gut. Our right tackle, Sweetpea's little brother Jackie, rammed his man back, and there it was, the crack of daylight Blaine needed. He had to get there, and he had to get there right now. But that knee sabotaged him from the get-go. You couldn't see it if you wasn't watching for it, but I knew he didn't get launched off as quick as he needed to. That hole in the line filled up with white jerseys and blue helmets faster than a summer storm taking over a clear sky, and there wasn't even a crack left for Blaine to shoot through.

Under my breath, I was telling him, *Go down, son. Just go down and take your medicine. Don't take no chances now.* But Blaine couldn't go down. This whole season, he'd come up short of the kind of football everybody was used to from him, and he had to make him a real statement before the season come unraveled on him like a third-string practice jersey.

He turned down along the line of scrimmage, heading for left end, but the Titans' big farm-boy linebacker had already charged that side. Dead end. Nothing to do but cut back the other way, but that damn bad knee went traitor on him again. By the time he got his balance back, it was too late. One Titan wrapped him up high and another busted his legs out low, and the football went spinning out across the ground like a loose hubcap after a three-car pileup.

There must've been eight men jumped on top of that ball, squirming like a bunch of copperheads on hot asphalt, and you couldn't tell till the officials pried the last one up who recovered it.

Wynette.

I could just about hear the air go whistling out of the fans on our side of the stadium. Blaine was still down, and he raised up slow, limping a little but trying to hide it, not wanting to give Coach Huff the least reason to set him out if we ever got the ball back.

Running out to take my position, I stopped him as the offense and defense crisscrossed paths. "You okay?"

He slapped my shoulder pad. "You get them assholes for me. You hear? I don't care what you have to do, but you get 'em."

I nodded, snapping my chin strap down. It was hard to get me mad for myself, but I could damn sure get mad for a friend.

Less than two minutes left now, but two minutes can seem like a hot-August hour at the end of a close game. One mistake and Wynette'd pick up enough yardage for even their rubber-legged kicker to score a field goal, send the game into overtime. A bigger mistake this close to the end zone, and they might even score a touchdown. Game over. The five-year winning streak down the toilet and our chance at being legends flushed down with it. It'd be the defense's fault, but everyone would hang the blame on Blaine for fumbling. That'd be too much. I knew him better than anyone, even his own family. He wasn't built for carrying a sack of rocks that heavy up and down the streets of Kennisaw for the rest of his life.

Taking up my middle linebacker spot, I knew Wynette had

to pass. The smart play would be to shoot a short one out to the sideline, get out of bounds, maybe move the chains, but something told me that old camel-faced Titans coach would think that was too obvious right now. They'd try and be too smart for their own good.

I was right.

The center snapped the ball on a quick count, and the quarterback swiveled towards the tailback, and that's when I stopped time again. The tailback froze behind the left tackle, the quarterback leaning towards him like he was going to hand the ball off. A surprise running play. Only it was a fake and I knew it. The guard was already starting to pull back, which he wouldn't do on a run—nobody would run off-tackle in this situation unless they was crazy or stupid.

No, they was pulling the same play they nearly fooled me on a while ago. No doubt about it.

The easy thing to do would be to just lay back and wait for the split end to cut across the middle and bat the pass down or maybe even intercept it, but right now wasn't about the easy thing. Blaine told me to get them suckers for him, and, by God, I was going to get them.

First, I charged in like I was aiming for the tailback, but instead I dodged right into the backfield. The guard seen me, but I flew past him before he could pull his cleats up out of the ground. The quarterback wasn't looking at nothing but that big fat clearing I left open in the middle of the field. He planted and cocked his arm, ready to fire off one of them perfect spirals over the line to number eighty-eight. Man oh man, he could taste him a touchdown, sweeter than apple pie with ice cream on top.

But it was too late.

He wasn't throwing no more touchdowns today. He wasn't about to turn my best friend's fumble into no giant sack of back-crushing rocks. I smashed into him at full speed, banging my helmet straight into his shoulder, busting through him as easy as one of them paper banners the team runs through at the first of the game. Then, there it was, the ball bouncing loose, springing up with perfect timing into my hands. I didn't even have to slow down. I just tucked that ball under my arm and blew towards the end zone like a cool breeze in July.

I didn't spike the ball or dance. That's not my style. I only turned and watched as them black Knights jerseys stampeded towards me, ready to smother me with congratulations. The band kicked into the fight song, and the stands boomed, "Hampton! Hampton! Hampton!"

Like I said, that kind of thing don't give me the big head, but if I could've stopped time right then, I would have. I'd have froze that exact moment right there, closed it up in my fist, and took it home to show what I done. Maybe that finally would've made a difference.

CHAPTER THREE

After the game, we was out on Main Street in Blaine's old Blazer, stopped at the light just south of Jolly Cone, and these girls in their little red Mustang squealed down the road going the other way.

"Did you see them girls' faces when I mooned 'em?" Jake said, laughing.

Blaine checked him out in the rearview mirror and said, "Hey, yank your britches up, asshole. I don't want your naked butt on my upholstery."

"Are you kidding me?" Jake said. "You spilled enough beer on these old seats last Saturday night. I don't think you're gonna have to worry about my butt germs for a good long time."

"Besides," Darnell said, "this has to be the oldest Blazer in the history of the world. I'll bet it's the first one off the assembly line."

It was our quarterback, Darnell Wills, and our wide receiver Jake Sweet in the backseat and me and Blaine up front. All of us fresh and clean from our postgame showers, large and in charge.

Blaine patted the dashboard and said, "Good old Citronella." Citronella was what he called the Blazer. "She might be ancient, but, by God, she's loyal. And I'll tell you what, she's got a good pedigree too. Her first owner was George Washington hisself, and he sold her off to Buffalo Bill and he sold her to Babe Ruth and he sold her to Elvis Presley."

That was Blaine for you. He always could lay it on thick.

"And old Elvis, he sold it to Emmitt Smith's daddy two months before he kicked the bucket on the bathroom floor at Graceland, and it was Emmitt sold it to me."

"You're full of it," Jake said.

"And on top of that, Citronella don't get jealous of all the girls I run in and out of that backseat back there."

Darnell had to laugh at that one. "Now you're really full of it."

"You ever seen anyone light a fart on fire?" Jake said.

"Yeah," I told him. "We seen you do it last week, and we didn't want to see it then."

Old Jake, he wasn't a half bad wide receiver, but he was always playing the fool. Sometimes he got on Blaine's nerves a little more than he done with the rest of us, especially this season.

"You fart on my seat, and I'll break your arm," Blaine told him, and he only barely sounded like he was exaggerating it.

"What's the matter?" Jake shot back. "You still bent out of shape about almost losing us the game tonight?"

Anybody but Jake would've known better than to say something like that to Blaine.

Without the least warning, Blaine stomped on the brake pedal, and Citronella fishtailed to a dead stop right there in the middle of Main. He stared his Blaine stare into the rearview mirror. "You get your britches up right now, son, or I'm climbing back there, and we'll see who gets bent out of shape."

This time there wasn't no exaggeration about it.

Jake tried staring his own stare back into the mirror, but it didn't hold up. "Jesus, Blaine, what's eating you? Can't you take a joke no more?" He started hitching up his jeans.

Blaine didn't bother to answer that but just kept aiming his double-barrel glare into the mirror till Jake got his belt buckled. Then he gave a nod, like, *Okay, you're off the hook for now*, and started back down the street again.

"Hell," Jake said. "No one's worried about losing any games anyways. Not when we got old Hamp in there." He reached over the seat and slapped my shoulder, but I just looked down at the dashboard. Last thing Blaine wanted to hear was how someone had to save his bacon.

"That's the truth," Darnell said. "You was amazing out there tonight, Hamp."

"Aw, I didn't do nothing the rest of you wouldn't have done." I caught myself rubbing my palm along the short bristles of hair on top of my head. It's kind of a nervous thing I do when I get embarrassed. Blaine told me one time it drove him crazy, made me look like I didn't have no self-confidence, so I tried to quit, but it kept coming back.

"Man oh man," Darnell said. "I mean, you straight-out laid it on that quarterback. He was stretched out down there on the ground so flat he looked about like some old piece of pizza you gotta peel up off the box with a knife. I'm sure glad you're on our team. I don't want no one laying me out like that."

"That ain't no lie," Jake said. "So tell me, Hamp, how's it feel to score an eighty-yard touchdown?"

I glanced over at Blaine. He didn't say nothing, but the way he was strangling that steering wheel, I could tell he was still pretty good and annoyed with old Jake.

"I don't know," I said. "Why don't you ask Blaine? He scored one eighty-five yards and some change."

"Aw," Darnell said. "That was all the way last season, though."

"That's right," Jake said. "This year it looks like he's gonna need you to bail him out if we're gonna get us another unde-feated season."

Jake don't know when to keep shut up.

Blaine didn't stomp on the brake this time, though. He just snorted like he couldn't hardly be bothered with some-thing so stupid. "That'll be the day," he said.

"I don't know," Jake kept on. "You better watch out or Hamp's gonna go off to OU without you, and you're gonna be stuck here riding up and down the strip and circling through Jolly Cone on Saturday nights right on through till you're sixty."

"Shoot," Blaine said. "Hampton's not mean enough for big-time college football. Not yet."

We'd talked about going over to Norman to the Univer-sity of Oklahoma together since we was in fifth grade, and this was the first time he'd said anything about how I wasn't mean enough for big-time college football. I didn't like it. Sure, he was irritated at Jake trying to get his goat, but I didn't see why he had to take it out on me none.

"What are you talking about?" I said. "Didn't you see me flatten that quarterback? I bet you he thought I was plenty mean enough."

Blaine smiled a little snickery smile. "Yeah, and I also seen you helping their man up on the sideline, patting him on the butt like he was your boyfriend too."

"All that is is sportsmanship," I said.

"It's soft is what it is. You can't let the enemy see you being weak. Ever. That's rule number one. You're a Knight, son. My dad told me back in his day, every team they played got scared just watching the Knights run on the field. It's the way they carried themselves. The swagger. That's how you keep on top. You can't let 'em see you look weak, and you can't let 'em see you hurt. And sometimes you have to be downright brutal. When it counts."

We rode along without saying nothing for a moment. It never even crossed my mind to bring up what would've happened if Wynette'd scored them a touchdown on top of his fumble. But that's the way it always was with Blaine. He could think up an argument for his side quicker than a rich man's lawyer, but me, I had to mull things over, look them up and down and inside out, so by the time I come up with an answer, there's no one around to tell but my bedpost.

"But don't worry, Hamp," Blaine said finally. "Come February first, when we finally get to set down and sign a National Letter of Intent, I'll make sure you sign on with OU right alongside me. We just gotta get a little more *mean* in you. You'll do just fine. Old Blaine'll look after you."

And I would've just let it lay right there, happy to get

things back on an even keel, or at least as even as things usually got with Blaine, but Jake had to throw one more stick on the fire.

"What are you talking about, Blaine? You ain't even heard from OU. Hamp'll do just fine on his own. And I'll bet he'll go wherever he wants, with folks like Harvey Warrick calling him up."

"Who?"

"Harvey Warrick. All-American linebacker five years ago for—"

"I know who he is," Blaine said. "Just about the best linebacker to ever come out of this state." He looked over at me. "What I'm wondering is why I ain't heard about this till right now."

"It ain't nothing official," I said. "He just wanted to tell me about his old college program and all like that."

I had to turn and look out the side window. It wasn't like I was trying to hide anything from Blaine, but I knew how he was. If any hotshot players was going to call anyone about college programs—even if they wasn't from OU—he was bound to figure they ought to be calling him first. Truth be known, I thought they ought to call him first too. He was the leader. Just 'cause his knee was dragging him down a little this year didn't change that.

"You better watch out for that kind of deal," he said. "That could be a recruiting violation right there. Alumni ain't supposed to be calling high school players during the regular season."

"Come on," Jake said. "I'll bet the boys up in the big Class 5A and 6A high schools are getting calls from alums right and left. Probably some's even getting calls from agents already."

Blaine shook his head. "If they are, they're in violation. The NCAA's got a whole stack of rules on who can contact you, when they can contact you, when you can go on official visits, and all that. There's what you call 'quiet periods' and 'dead periods' when you can't hardly have any contact. Coaches, assistant coaches, boosters, alums—there's different restrictions for all of 'em. I oughta know. My dad made me take a test over it. I had to study and everything. He graded it just like it was for school. It's the only test I ever made an A on too."

"Well, whoop-de-do for you," Jake said. "Having rules and actually going by 'em is two different things. The only reason Hampton ain't getting flooded with calls from the big boys is 'cause we're stuck in piddly little 4A. But I'll tell you what, Hamp. You don't need Blaine to put a word in for you. You'll do just fine on your own. By the end of the season, you'll have everyone in Oklahoma and Texas ringing you up. I don't care how far we are from the big-city newspapers—you can't keep five undefeated seasons off the sports page."

"I guess," I said, but I couldn't get excited about it like Jake. It just hadn't dawned on me before that me and Blaine might not both get picked to go to the same college, and I wasn't anywheres near sure I could make it up at some big-time school by myself.

Blaine didn't say nothing more about it, though. He didn't say nothing at all. He just stared through that dusty windshield down at the dark end of Main Street.

CHAPTER FOUR

The cramped little rent house I lived in with my mom was almost to the end of Mission Road, not exactly the bad side of town but a long way from Ninth Street Hill, where all the big white houses was. Blaine pulled Citronella up to the curb, and I got out and told the boys to take it easy. There was a light on in the living room window radiating off a warm yellow glow, but it didn't give me any good old homey-type feeling. It was more of a what's-it-gonna-be-this-time? feeling instead. That was a pretty familiar one by now.

Up on the front porch, I could hear the stereo playing inside. Fleetwood Mac. My mom loved Fleetwood Mac. Didn't matter that they was about as ancient as a bunch of Egyptian mummies, she never got tired of them. There wasn't anything to do, though, but open up the door and go in, so that's what I done. Sure enough, she had her a man in there, another new one.

They was over on the other side of the couch, slow dancing, even though it wasn't a slow song playing. He was short, with a Hawaiian shirt. She had one hand on his shoulder and he had one on her hip, and in their other hands they was both holding these jelly-jar glasses with golden brown liquid sloshing up against the sides. An open whiskey bottle set on the coffee table and you could smell the sharp-sweet odor of it from clear across the room.

"Oh, hi, honey," she said, not bothering to unwrap herself off Mr. Hawaiian Shirt long enough to even pretend nothing was going on. "Is the game over already?"

"It's been over two hours."

"I'm sorry I didn't make it to watch you play. I just got off work a little while ago."

I glanced back at the bottle on the table. It looked like more than just a little while's worth of whiskey was drained off to me. Not that my mom was an alcoholic or anything like that. She only drank a lot if the man she ran around with did. That was how she was. Every time she took up with someone new, she'd change herself to go along with him. And ever since my dad run off on us, she done a lot of taking up with someone new.

"How'd y'all do?" she asked. "Win as usual?"

"Yeah, we won."

"I'll bet you were the star too."

"Well," I said, making the mistake of thinking she was really interested in anything I done, "there was this one play—"

"Oh, where are my manners?" she cut in. "I haven't even introduced you and Jim. Jim, this is my son, Hampton. Hampton, this is Jim, uh, Jim . . ."

"Houck," he said, sounding about like he was hacking up a chunk of lung. "Jim Houck. I'm sales manager over at Butler Ford in Lowery." He let loose of my mom long enough to reach out his hand, and I gave it a shake. It was cold and damp from holding the drink, but that didn't stop him from trying one of them extra-firm grips to show me how even though I was a football player, he was more than a match for me in the strength department. He must've been a good eight inches shorter than me and wore these glasses that was too big for his face. They was a sporty style, though, and I figured he had hisself pictured as some kind of hotshot playboy.

"It was the funniest thing," Mom said, tacking on her little girly giggle. She was kind of young and girly still, I guess, with her bobbed-off blond hair, button nose, and petite figure, but still, a flirty little giggle just don't sound right coming out of your mom. "There I was working at the store and happened to look up, and who do you think came strolling in?"

It wasn't something I hadn't heard before, but it was still more than I wanted to know.

"So, did you say you made some sort of big play at the game tonight?" Jim Houck said, adjusting his sporty, hotshot glasses so as to give me a good once-over.

"Nothing too big," I said, not caring one way or the other what Jim Houck thought.

"You look all wore out, honey," Mom said then. "Why don't you go on back to your room now and get some rest." She waved her jelly-jar glass back towards the bedroom like maybe I forgot how to get back there or something.

"Yeah, sure," I said. "Sounds good." And it did sound good too. Sleep would've felt just fine.

In the bedroom, I eased my clothes off around the leftover pains from the game without even bothering to turn on the light. Laying down on top of the covers, I stared up into the dark, thinking about how the game went, rerunning every big play, building up to that moment at the end when them cheers busted loose and come pouring down like a big fat rain on some thirsty little broke-tail desert rat.

But sleep wouldn't come, not with Fleetwood Mac and Jim Houck playing that same old familiar tune in the living room, and the cheers faded out of my head. The good memory sank under the bad thoughts. Thoughts of what would happen if we didn't win out the season or if me and Blaine ended up not getting picked to play at the same college. Or if we didn't get picked to play football anywhere at all. And then it was just me, laying there in the dark alone.

CHAPTER FIVE

Was a time I never would've thought twice about anything coming between me and Blaine. Like I said, him and his dad got me into football in the first place, and Mr. Keller taught me how to hunt and fish and all sorts of stuff I never done before. Some weeks, I was over at their house more than I was at my own. But things had been changing this year, and maybe since longer ago than that.

Course, Blaine's knee injury got him frustrated, and seemed like he was always taking it out on the closest handy thing—which a lot of times was me—but that wasn't the only difference. I couldn't have told you what else it was, though, to save my life. You know how when you see someone day in, day out, year after year, you don't really notice him getting taller or wider or older or whatever? It can be like that with the way people are on the inside too.

Me and Blaine had been friends since we was nine years old. Met on the Fourth of July. It was one of them long summer days when the sun's blazing on high beam and the grass is still cow-pasture green, thick and long around the tree bottoms, way before it gets burned off to a scorched yellow like it does in the dry days of August when you know summer's running out on you. It was also the first day, far as I can remember, that I ever made time stop.

I'd only lived in Kennisaw for about a month after moving down from Poynter, which is a little town about fifty miles to the north. It was a pretty fine old town. I had me plenty of friends and got along real good with my folks, especially my mom. She wasn't always like she was now. Used to be, my mom was about my best friend. Wasn't nothing I couldn't talk to her about back in them Poynter days. And talk about funny. She could crack a joke with the best of them, at least up till that day I come home from school to find her setting on the wood front porch by herself.

Her face was washed-out pale, and there was tearstains striping down her cheeks plain as skid marks on a dead-end road. That wasn't right. My mom was a laugher, a teaser and a tickler and a bathroom singer. She only cried at black-and-white movies.

I asked her what was the matter, and she kind of stuttered around before finally she come out with how my dad up and run off. Moved to Sapulpa and wouldn't be coming back no more. Even took the lawn mower with him. Then she drew her top lip in tight and said that was all right with her. That was just fine, 'cause it didn't pay to try and count on people anyways. I waited around for her to say something else, give some explanation about why he left, but she never done it.

26

Later on it come out that he run off with this little eighteen-year-old Barbie doll he met installing cable TV at her parents' house. My aunt told me that. She never had liked my dad. Or me neither, I don't guess.

Wasn't long before Mom got sick of walking around Poynter and having to look at all the stuff that reminded her of Dad, so she got a job at the dollar store here in Kennisaw. We moved down the very weekend after school let out. Now here it was, the Fourth of July, and so far I hadn't done nothing but wander the streets and vacant lots by myself, talking to the ants and horny toads. We didn't even have money for fireworks. I did have one thing to look forward to, though. They was having an outdoor ceremony down at Leonard Biggins Park, and who do you think was going to be the guest of honor but old T. Roy Strong, the ex-All-Pro from off the Dallas Cowboys.

As far as football stars from Oklahoma went, you couldn't get much bigger than T. Roy. Talk about your legends. T. Roy played quarterback for Kennisaw back in their famous undefeated days and went on from there to land runner-up to the Heisman Trophy as a college star, and as if that wasn't enough, he got drafted by the Dallas Cowboys in the first round and ended up helping them win the Super Bowl not once but twice. Now here he was, back with a pack of his old Kennisaw teammates to honor what a lot of folks called the greatest high school football team in the history of the eastern Oklahoma hill country.

So, taking my shortcut down through a grove of trees on my way to the park, I was pretty excited, daydreaming up how it would be to talk to T. Roy Strong. I even got so far as picturing us tossing a football around and telling each other about our lives. Not just piddly things about where we was from and what kind of ice cream we liked, but deep things. Like what a father and son would talk about.

Then, all the sudden, this kid dropped down out of a tree right in front of me. Just—*boom!*—there he was. It was Blaine, but course, I didn't know that then. For all I knew, he could've been something from outer space zapping out of the sky.

"Halt there, knave," he said, planting his hands on his hips. "Where doth thou thinkest thou art fixing to go?" Even way back then, he was broad shouldered and had him a deep tan and dark brown eyes and black hair that stuck up on top of his head like he hadn't combed it a day since school let out for summer. Nine years old and he already looked like he ought to be the star of something.

"What'd you call me?" I said. I hadn't never heard the word *knave*, and I wanted to make sure he wasn't calling me any bad names.

"*Knave,*" he said, like he'd heard some dumb questions but that one was the topper. "That means thou ain't a member of my kingdom."

"Who are you anyways?" The way he was talking, I thought he might be from another country.

"Me? I'm Sir Galahad. Who the hell art thou?"

"I'm Batman."

He grinned his big old shiny white grin and said, "Why, hell, this here's fixing to be the battle of the century, then." And he bucked his head down and charged straight at my belly with no more warning than a bobcat gives a weasel.

Right there was when I done it. Froze him solid in his tracks. It was almost like I was looking down on the both of us, figuring just what I had to do, and then—*click*—everything rolled into motion again. I dodged off to one side and at the same time grabbed ahold of Blaine's T-shirt at the shoulder, wrenching him around so's he couldn't hit me square on. Then, before he could figure out what was what, I tackled him like he thought he was fixing to do me, and we went tumbling down the side of this steep hill there, rolling over and over each other, ending up in the tall grass at the bottom.

As quick as we hit bottom, I sprung up on one knee, ready for some more combat, but Blaine—he just laid back in that high grass and laughed out loud. "Boy howdy," he said. "Where you from anyways?"

"I'm from here," I said, still not one hundred percent sure the fighting was over.

"Nuh-uh," he said. "You can't be from here. I'm from here, and I ain't never seen you before."

I explained how I just moved to town and my mom worked at the dollar store, and he kind of checked me over with his eyes squinted up and said, "Well, that's different, then. As long as you're a Kennisaw boy, we can be friends."

And we shook on it right then and there—Fourth of July, bottom of the hill, east side of Leonard Biggins Park.

Turned out, we both come over for the same reason, to see T. Roy Strong, and Blaine made sure we got prime seats in a big white oak just to the side of the pavilion where the ceremony was supposed to take place. Now, I didn't know that much about T. Roy's high school career back then, just that he was the top-dog legend all over eastern Oklahoma, but Blaine knew the facts on him from Genesis to Revelation, and he didn't mind sharing them while we waited up in that tree for the ceremony to kick off.

The deal was, over ten years before me and Blaine was even born, the Kennisaw Knights football team only lost three games in an eight-year run. Six of them years, they went undefeated, with five of them six being straight in a row, just like we'd have a chance of doing later on. And out of all the great players to wear the black and gold, T. Roy Strong was the greatest. Bar none. He was a three-year starter at quarterback and could outrun, outthrow, and outthink any other high school quarterback in the country. Some said you might as well include college in there too 'cause T. Roy was that good.

He held either division or state records in five categories, and one time he threw a touchdown pass out of his own end zone with his foot an inch from the back line. A one-hundred-and-nine-yard and thirty-five-inch touchdown pass! Another time he run a quarterback sneak to gain two feet and ended up on the other side of the goal line, eighty-five yards away. Got his picture all the way up in the Tulsa paper after that one.

But his most amazing play happened in the state title game his senior year. He had these three triple-large linemen chasing him all over the backfield, nipping at his heels like grizzlies on a jackrabbit, so what did he do? He launched the ball, on purpose, straight into the helmet of the biggest one of them. *Pow!* The ball popped up at least twenty foot high, and when it come down, T. Roy snatched it out of the air and streaked down the sideline and all the way to the end zone, untouched. That one made the national news: QUARTERBACK CATCHES OWN TOUCHDOWN PASS!

T. Roy Strong. They played offense and defense back then, and he even run back punts on special teams. You could still go up to the cliffs above Lake Hawkshaw outside of town and see where girls carved out their declarations of love for him in the rock. When he went pro with Dallas, they shifted him over to cornerback, and he had to retire after only six seasons with a bad shoulder, but that didn't matter. He was still a Dallas Cowboy, a Pro Bowl pick, a Super Bowl winner, and hands-down Kennisaw, Oklahoma's favorite son. No question.

And I guarantee when he walked out on the stage in that little pavilion in front of me and Blaine, he still looked every inch the hero too. Except for the smooth way he moved, he could've been a town-square statue with that rock jaw and perfect haircut and slick gray suit. The crowd just about come out of their skin from cheering so hard. Behind him, six other big walking statues lined up, all members of the same team as T. Roy, the greatest of all the great Knights teams of the olden days.

I never will forget the speech he gave that July Fourth, and I know Blaine won't neither. Right there, that was what it meant to be a Kennisaw Knight. He stepped up to the microphone and raised his hands to get the crowd to simmer down, bowing his head at first, real modest, then raising it back up and flashing that big wide perfect smile of his that let you know he was as glad to see you as he would be to see the president of the United States.

"Thank you," he said. "Thank each and every one of you who came out to help honor one of the greatest groups of guys anyone ever had the opportunity to play a game of football or any other kind of game with."

The whoops and clapping busted loose again, and he lifted his hands back up to quiet us down before going on. "It humbles me to stand here before this wonderful crowd of fans and alongside my old teammates, who have all gone on to accomplish great things. But we're not here to talk about that right now. We're here to talk about days past, a different time. A time when giants walked the Earth."

The crowd couldn't help but let out another roar, and me and Blaine looked each other in the eye, both of us nodding, not having to say a word about how big a moment it was we was witnessing in front of us.

T. Roy went on then, reeling off all the team's big triumphs, the hard work they put in, the adversity they faced, and the unbreakable bonds they forged. For a second there, he even cried a little. Right out in the open. Anyone littler might've got ridiculed for doing something like that in public, but everyone just loved T. Roy more for it. He'd learned the meaning of courage, he said, and strength and comradeship. He'd reached the top of a mountain and stretched up his hands and felt the warmth of God shining down on his face, as if to say, "T. Roy, job well done."

"And so, in conclusion," he said, "I hope all you here in Kennisaw, in this small town in the Oklahoma hills, will remember the greatness that lies within. Stick together. Do good, and then push yourself to do even better. The Knights of the hill country stand for honor and integrity, inner fortitude and grit, and the triumph that comes from hard work, and all of you here are a part of that magnificent tradition!"

The crowd boomed so loud then that every bird in every tree around that pavilion launched up into the air at the same time, hundreds of them, soaring up and up, like they was a mirror of the way all of us was feeling down below.

Blaine looked at me and said, as serious as if he was reciting off the Pledge of Allegiance, "That's the way I'm gonna be one of these days. Just like that."

"Me too," I said, every bit as serious.

CHAPTER SIX

Course, Blaine wasn't up there with T. Roy, even before his knee injury, but if you didn't know him like me, you'd have swore he thought he was, the way he strutted cocky as hell down senior hall on Monday after that Wynette game. Like a flying ace come back from war after saving his country. And that was all right. Just being a Kennisaw Knight made you a hero in our town. Up and down Main Street, old men was always slapping us on the backs and shaking our hands, telling us to keep up the good work. Make Kennisaw proud. At school, you couldn't hardly get to class on time for folks, students and teachers both, coming up to tell you, "Good game."

But truth be told, that kind of stuff always felt awkward to me, uncomfortable, like wearing a heavy coat that really belonged to somebody else. Thing was, away from tackles and passes and dodging blockers, I didn't have the least idea how to stop time and look two seconds ahead and know what to do. I didn't understand why it was, but outside the stadium, gravity was different. Walking around them high school halls, I felt as heavy and slow as a big old Clydesdale stomping around in a herd of quarter horses. Even with folks telling me how great I played against Wynette, I couldn't do nothing but sort of shrug, rub my hand across the top of my head, and say thanks, while Blaine could stand there and talk for fifteen minutes, people he'd known all his life grinning at him like he was a movie star. Man, I wished I could be that way.

Blaine took up his usual spot, leaning against the senior-hall lockers with his thumbs in his belt loops, and I stood next to him, trying not to look so big and redheaded. "Check out them jeans," he said, nodding towards Darla Monroe as she walked away down the hall in her skintight Rockies. "Did you see how tight them things was? I could just about read the label on her underwear through there."

"Yeah," I said, but I wasn't really paying much attention. Instead, I looked off towards the door of my homeroom, thinking of someone besides Darla.

"Damn, son," Blaine said. "You didn't hardly look at her."

"I've seen her before."

"I'll tell you what, we better get you a girlfriend before people start thinking there's something wrong with you."

"What if there ain't nobody I really like all that much, though?"

"It don't matter if you like 'em. They just have to look good. Remember when we drove over to OU to look around campus? All the big dogs there had the best-looking women.

That's just one of your natural rights when you're a football player. Why, when T. Roy Strong played down in Dallas, they say he went out with a new girl every night. Now, that's the way it oughta be."

"I don't know about that," I said. Down the hall, Sara Reynolds come walking around the corner, heading for history class. I started that way myself. "I'll talk to you later. It's time for class."

"What's your hurry? Hang around and watch the scenery go by with me for a while."

"See ya at lunch." I didn't even turn back. There wasn't no use trying to explain Sara Reynolds to Blaine.

She was already in her usual desk when I walked into class and slid into my seat in the next row over, a yard or two behind her. She had a way of setting there with her back real straight and her ankles crossed and her hands folded on the desktop that made a perfect picture. About all the skin you could see on her was them little fingers barely sticking out from the sleeves of her big baggy sweatshirt, but that was all right. Sometimes I'd just stare at them fingers. Mr. Foudy, the history teacher, started in saying something, but it wasn't about Sara Reynolds, so I didn't really give a day-old donut what it was.

You think I felt awkward clomping down the hall with people congratulating me right and left, treating me like I was different somehow? Well, that wasn't nothing compared to how it was when it come to schoolwork and girls. What I wouldn't have gave to stop time and see the right thing to do with them two.

Taking tests was terrible. During class, dates and names and terms would go floating out of my reach like cottonwood

35

feathers blowing off on the wind, and it'd only be later, way after school let out, the right answer would light back down on my shoulder. But what can you do? It's not like I could call the teacher up at nine o'clock at night and say, "Hello there, Mr. Foudy? This is Hampton Green, and you know that question number twenty-three on the test today? The one about where old Robert E. Lee did his surrendering at? I just remembered the answer was supposed to be Appomattox, Virginia. Thanks. See ya tomorrow."

Wasn't no teacher living or dead that'd buy a deal like that.

But worse even than the tests was girls. Nothing like a girl to turn me right into a fool. My friends didn't care none what kind of grades I made, but there wasn't no letup on the hard time they gave me about how bad I was with girls. Sometimes I would've traded just about everything I done on the football field just to know the right thing to say to the right girl, but when it come to flirting, it might as well have been French, for all I could understand of it.

Sara Reynolds wasn't exactly the type any of my friends would look at as prime girlfriend material for a Kennisaw Knight, though. Especially Blaine. She was real smart, took advanced chemistry and violin lessons, and seemed kind of shy most of the time, except when she disagreed with something a teacher said. Look out then. None of that stuff's likely to get a girl elected prom queen anytime this century, but I didn't care. There was just something about her.

It didn't have nothing to do with a pair of tight Rockies neither. Her jeans was every bit as baggy as them sweatshirts she always wore. I swear, you couldn't tell whuther her body had started developing any more shape to it senior year than back when she first showed up in Kennisaw during eighth grade.

And it sure wasn't that hair of hers. Now, I don't want to sound like I didn't think she was cute, 'cause I did, but even she'd probably admit her hair wouldn't land her on no magazine covers, not with how she just parted it in the middle and let it run wild from there. The way it was, that cute little pale face of hers looked about like it was peeking out through some kind of crazy brown shrub that the biology books hadn't got around to classifying yet. On humid days it was a whole jungle.

Back in junior high, the boys traipsed along behind her in the hall, asking her dumb questions like when was the robins coming back to roost in that nest she had on her head. "Farmer Brown called," they'd say in their singsongy way. "He wants his haystack back." Then somebody come up with the nickname Bush Girl. It never caught on too good, though, since she wouldn't never get mad about it. She'd just shake her head and look at them boys with that sad expression in her big brown Sara Reynolds eyes. Not sad for herself—nuh-uh—but sad for them boys and their foolishness.

And that was it. That was the thing about Sara Reynolds, them sad, soulful brown eyes. I noticed them from day one but never figured they had much to do with me till a few weeks back when she come up after class and talked to me about the massacres.

What happened was, I got in some trouble for asking Mr. Foudy how come every time the Indians won a battle back in the Old West days, it got called a massacre, and every time the cavalry won, they called it a victory. Usually, I ain't one for talking up in class, but I'd been mulling this deal over for about a week, and it just didn't seem fair to me. But after the class got to laughing, I guess old Mr. Foudy thought I was trying to be some kind of troublemaker.

"Well, Hampton," he said, smiling his sweet fake smile. "In case you haven't noticed, we have quite a few Native American students here in our school, and I'm sure they don't appreciate your insinuation, so maybe in the future you'll think twice before making your smart remarks."

I could feel myself turning red as the inside of a thermometer on that one. I wasn't trying to make any kind of smart remark or insinuation, either one. But what could I do? It took me a good week to figure out the question, I couldn't no more come up with an answer to shoot off to Mr. Foudy right there on the spot than I could've recited the Gettysburg Address backwards while holding a lit match.

So the rest of the period, I set there and stewed. I figured the class only laughed 'cause they wasn't used to me talking out much, but Mr. Foudy should've known better. It wasn't right for him to get any of my Native American friends in the class to thinking I was trying to make fun of them when it was really just the opposite. I was still stewing on it when Sara walked up to me after class.

"Hampton," she said, tugging on my sleeve. "I just wanted you to know I understood what you meant."

"You did?" I looked down into them eyes, and, boy howdy, that was it for me right there.

"And I agree with you," she said.

"You do?"

"Yes."

"Really?"

That was the best I could come up with to say, so she finally just said she'd see me later and walked off. But the way she looked at me, it was like she seen something in me nobody else did. I wasn't sure what it was she seen, but it felt good, like stepping out on the porch on a summer morning and it's already warm. A whole new day waiting on you. Course, that wasn't something I could tell her. I could bowl over a hundred blockers and plow down quarterback after quarterback, but I couldn't hardly say two words to this little five-foot-four-inch-tall girl.

Today in class wasn't any different. The whole time Mr. Foudy was going on about the Civil War, I was trying out imaginary conversations with Sara that I was pretty sure would never really happen. It wasn't till he called on us to circle up our desks and get into our study groups that he caught my attention.

For my money, study groups was one of the all-time great inventions in teaching. For one reason: me and Sara was assigned to the same one. Time after time, we gathered up with my buddy Darnell and the world's worst drum majorette, Lana Pitt, and every time, I told myself I was going to come up with the perfect thing to say to Sara. Something clever and flirty but not mushy. Only every time, my head wouldn't do nothing but turn into a big chunk of petrified wood. Today was going to be different, though, I told myself. Today was the day.

We had us a fifty-item worksheet on the Civil War, and I pretended to try to look up the answers while everybody else really found them. But I couldn't think of one single clever-and-flirty-but-not-mushy thing to say. Problem was, Darnell and Lana was making too much racket arguing. Darnell didn't see how nobody with an ounce of brains could fight for the Confederates, and Lana said she had ancestors that was on the South's side and they was fighting for a way of life and old-fashioned family values.

Darnell turned over to me. "Can you believe this girl, Hamp? You explain it to her. I'm wore out."

"I don't know that much about it," I said, looking down. Last thing I wanted to do was get balled up in a controversy. As good a fighter as I was on the football field, I hated an argument in civilian life. Darnell was my best friend after Blaine and he was black, so I wasn't about to take the South's side, but I didn't want to hurt Lana's feelings neither. Besides, I didn't know but what Sara might have some relatives from the South somewheres along the line too.

Darnell threw up his hands. "How about you, Sara? You're smart. Let me ask you. Was slavery wrong?"

"Of course," she said.

"Well, then, let me ask you another thing. What reason could anybody have for fighting on a side that wants to own slaves?"

Sara was quiet for a moment, her long eyelashes shading down over her eyes. "Well," she said finally, "I guess a lot of folks want to be part of a side so much they just go along with what their side says is right."

"Even when it's really wrong," Darnell threw in.

"That's just it," Sara said. "Some people don't know who they really are themselves, so how are they going to know what they think is right or wrong?"

Darnell and Lana both said something back to that, but I didn't listen. I was still mulling over what Sara just said. It seemed like the wisest thing I'd ever heard someone my own age come up with. Talk about hitting home. Man. Last year, it wouldn't have meant nothing to me. I knew exactly who I was then. I was a Kennisaw Knight. But now that my Knights days was numbered, I could've stood to have that saying of hers etched in fancy writing on a wood-frame mirror and hung up over my bedroom dresser so I could look at it every morning before school.

Darnell and Lana was still jabbering when something unexpected happened. Mr. Foudy announced that class was almost over, and if we wasn't done with our worksheets, we'd have to finish up after school. That's when it come. The perfect idea. Only I wasn't the one to think of it.

"How about this," Sara said. "We could get together sometime this evening and if we split the questions up even between us, we could get done in thirty minutes."

There it was, just that easy. I'd been working so hard on coming up with my clever-flirty deal that I done completely overlooked something as simple as getting together to study after school. It really was perfect. I could see how it'd be. Me and Sara setting side by side on the sofa, only without none of the pressure I had the few measly times my friends fixed me up with girls they thought was right for me. It wouldn't just be the two of us struggling around to make conversation neither. We'd have Darnell and Lana and the good old Civil War worksheet to take up the slack.

Problem was, Darnell had to watch his younger brothers and sisters after football practice, and Lana had dance over at Miss Nikomos's studio. "I'm in modern dance," she said, looking at me like I was supposed to be impressed by that.

I turned over to Sara and said, "Sounds good to me," so fast I even surprised myself.

Darnell raised his eyebrows. Lana scrunched her nose up.

CHAPTER SEVEN

Now, if you never been a teenage boy, you might think the first thing I done was run and tell my best friend how great it was about going over to Sara Reynolds's house, but everybody else knows better. I wouldn't no more have told Blaine about me and Sara than I'd have stuck my nose down a garbage disposal.

At lunch, we took our regular table up by the north door of the cafeteria. It was meat loaf day. Blaine rocked back in his chair, going on and on with one of his funny stories about a prank he played on some little unsuspecting sophomore. The story was a long one with a couple extra curlicues added in here and there for special effects, but I kept fading out of it, thinking instead about how it'd be over at Sara's later on.

The way I pictured it, the two of us would be setting there

on the couch, leaning in close so we could read each other's Civil War worksheets. Our hands would touch every time we went to turn a page in the history book. For good measure, I had us down in a basement that Sara's folks converted into a TV room or something. Seemed like a lot of my friends had stories about girls and places like that. I never knew so many people even had converted basements.

Down on the imaginary couch, I was confident and smooth as old James Bond hisself. I knew just what to say. I pulled back that hair of hers and stared into her soulful-sad brown eyes and told her there wasn't no one else anywheres in the world like her.

"Hampton," she'd tell me. "I've had a crush on you since all the way back in junior high."

"What if your parents come downstairs?" I'd ask.

"Oh, they never come down," she'd say with a playful little glint in her eyes.

We wouldn't need no more words then. She'd know me, and I'd know her, and there wouldn't be no holding back anymore.

Just then, Darnell laid his lunch tray down on the table. "So, Hamp," he said. "Looks like you have yourself a date with Sara Reynolds tonight."

If he'd set my hair on fire, it couldn't have been any worse than saying that right in front of Blaine.

"A date?" Blaine rocked forward with a thud. "With *who?*"

Usually, he didn't like his stories interrupted, but this news was too big to pass up.

"It's not a date," I said. "It's just some history homework we gotta finish up."

He shook his head at me like I was just a real pitiful specimen. "Surely you can get someone better to copy your home-work off of than Bush Girl."

"I ain't copying off her," I said. "And don't call her Bush Girl."

"Uh-huh, so you *do* like her."

I looked down at what was left of my meat loaf, but I could feel Blaine staring at the top of my head. "Sure, I like her. She's nice. But that don't mean—"

Blaine slapped the table so hard the silverware rattled. "No way. I ain't gonna let you get hooked up with some little bushy-headed geek like that."

"She ain't a geek," I said.

"No, you're right. She don't even qualify as a geek. She's just a pure nobody."

"Hey now," Darnell cut in. "Everybody's somebody. Be-sides, what's the big deal? Hamp's too backwards to try any-thing with her anyways." He gave me a playful punch in the shoulder the way guys always done when they was putting me down on how bad I was with girls.

"I never said I was gonna try nothing with her," I told him. "All we're gonna do is finish up a history worksheet. So let's just drop it, okay?"

Blaine wasn't about to let it loose, though. Not for a sec-ond. He had to go on and lay out a whole sermon on how he couldn't let his best friend and the best defensive player on the best football team in the state start tagging around with an inferior product like Sara Reynolds. "Hampton," he said, "don't you know we're like the damn royalty at this school? You gotta step up and act like it, son. I'll tell you what, I'll get Rachel to hook you up with one of her friends."

"I don't need you doing that," I said. Rachel Calloway was

Blaine's girlfriend and probably the best-looking girl in our high school, which was saying something at our school with all the good-lookers we had around. Most of them was Rachel's friends too, but I didn't have the least thing in common with a one of them, as far as I could see. Besides, truth was, they about scared me to death.

"How about Kim Hunt?" Darnell suggested.

"No, we tried her already," Blaine said. "Hampton spilled a bowl of chili on her."

"Hey," I said. "I tripped and she just happened to be setting right there."

"Wait a minute." Blaine snapped his fingers and grinned a jackpot-winner grin. "I got the perfect candidate. Misty Koonce."

I about choked on my meat loaf over that one. If Rachel Calloway was Kennisaw's top beauty queen, then Misty was first runner-up.

"Misty Koonce?" Darnell said. "I thought she was dating some guy from over in Lowery."

"That's right," I said. "She never dates guys from our school. I think it's like a rule she has."

"She dumped that Lowery guy," Blaine said. "Yes sir, this is perfect. I guarantee, this Saturday night, Hamp, it's gonna be me and Rachel and you and Misty Koonce on a double date."

"I don't know," I said. "Misty Koonce?"

Blaine leaned back in his chair, real satisfied with hisself. "It's as good as done."

CHAPTER EIGHT

After football practice, I had just enough time to heat me up a couple of leftover hamburger patties and some macaroni before making the long walk over to Sara's. Mom was either still working at the dollar store or out somewheres with Jim Houck, the hotshot car dealer. She didn't leave a note, so I didn't know for sure. I wasn't even sure if she'd gave old Jim his walking papers yet. That was her usual routine. Dump the guy before he had a chance to dump her like my father done. Sure, she'd put on a good act for a while, but an act's all it was. Sometimes I wondered what would happen if she ever run across a real good guy, someone just right for her, if she'd even be able to tell the difference.

I sure wasn't someone to judge on that score, though. The more I studied on what Blaine said at lunch, the more confused I got about which girl I ought to go out with. Maybe he was right. Maybe Sara wasn't the one for me. To hear Blaine tell it, you'd think I was letting him and the whole football team down just by liking her. And anyone would have to be crazy to turn down a date with Misty Koonce.

Misty was blond and popular and cute in that official way girls was supposed to be cute. You sure didn't have to guess about how much her body had filled out neither. Wasn't a guy at our school that hadn't spent a good chunk of time running pictures of Misty through his head, especially if he ever seen her out at Lake Hawkshaw leaning up against Buddy Shiff's bass boat in that little macramé-looking bikini.

It was a sure thing if I had me a girl like Misty on my arm, my buddies would have to stop giving me a hard time about being backwards in the sex department. I didn't know how the hell they got so educated on the subject anyways. They was my age. I'd grown up with most of them. How did they turn into sex encyclopedias all the sudden? Course, I couldn't ask them about it outright. You never admit you don't know anything about a subject like that even if it's the most obvious thing in the world you don't.

Misty or Sara. Sara or Misty. Them two girls kept rolling around in my head like dice in a leather cup. On the one hand, Misty was just the type you'd think a football player ought to go out with. While on the other hand, Sara, well, she was just Sara. If there was a high school book of how things was supposed to be, the way I felt about her wasn't likely to be listed. And you could bet old T. Roy Strong never dated someone folks called Bush Girl neither.

The whole long walk over to Sara's house, I run these ideas through my head back and forth and every which ways, but I still didn't have it sorted out by the time I stepped up on her porch. Even after I rung the doorbell, I felt about like jumping over the banister and sprinting down the street for home. Then she opened the door and shined them soulful-sad brown eyes out at me, and I remembered why she was different from Misty Koonce.

"Hey," she said, brushing her hair back from her face.

"Hey." I looked down at the green welcome mat and told myself to forget what anybody else said about the subject of girls. "Hope I'm not late."

"No, you're right on time. Come on in."

Soon as I stepped through her door, things was different from what I was used to with my regular friends. For one, it smelled like rocks in there. And they did—they used rocks for decorations. Had them on little tables and shelves all the way from the front hall to all over the living room. Big black rocks, little gray ones, red ones and white ones and every kind of shape you'd ever want in a rock. They looked good and they smelled good, clean and hard.

Sara caught me admiring them. "My parents are geologists," she said.

And she took me right in to talk to them too, instead of steering me off to another room the way a lot of kids will do, like their parents have some kind of disease that'd strike you down with a deadly case of boredom if you hung around them too much.

Sara, she just leaned up against the side of the sofa next to her mother as comfortable as could be and even introduced her parents by their first names like I was fixing to be one of their buddies. Made me feel like someone worth knowing.

Mr. Reynolds—I couldn't call him Mark even if he was introduced that way—was parked in a wheelchair next to the

49

sofa and had him a guitar cradled on his lap. He didn't look like no one else in Kennisaw, and not just 'cause of the wheelchair neither. He had a little ponytail and a goatee and wore a black beret. I'd never seen anyone wearing a beret outside of TV. Course, I'd noticed him rolling around town before, but I never knew he was Sara's dad. It's funny, but even in a town of 9,500 people like Kennisaw, there can be whole different circles of folks. Whole different worlds, almost.

Mrs. Reynolds—who Sara introduced as Nancy—looked about like she could've been Sara's big sister. Wore the same kind of comfortable baggy clothes, and there wasn't no mistaking where Sara got all her hair from. Her mom couldn't have been more friendly to me neither, just like Mr. Reynolds was. You'd think it never even crossed their minds to suspect how much time I'd done spent conjuring up pictures of their daughter on a converted-basement sofa with her sweatshirt and jeans tossed off on the floor.

What I figured was they must've been keeping track of my football-playing in the *Kennisaw Sun*. I didn't know why else they'd bother being so nice to someone they didn't even know. That part wasn't different from just about every other adult I run into around town. Always beating me over the head with football questions. How bad was the Knights going to whip Sawyer or Okalah or Kiowa Bluff? Who did I want to play college ball for, OU or OSU? Was I planning on playing in Dallas and winning me as many Super Bowl rings as T. Roy Strong? It got pretty old, if you want to know the truth.

So I wasn't surprised when Mrs. Reynolds come out and said how Sara'd told her I was on the football team.

"Yes, ma'am, I play linebacker," I said, getting ready for the same old questions.

"That's nice," she said with a smile. "How's the team doing?"

"Uh," I said. I sure wasn't ready for that one. Everyone in Kennisaw knew the Knights was working on their fifth undefeated season in a row. I thought they did, anyways.

Mr. Reynolds chuckled. "She doesn't follow sports much." He turned to his wife. "They're doing very well, dear. Undefeated, I believe?" He looked back at me, and I nodded.

"So," he said. "You play linebacker."

"Yes, sir."

Mr. Reynolds studied on that a moment. "Is that the person who stands behind the quarterback?"

"Not exactly," I said. "The linebacker's on defense." I glanced back and forth from Mr. Reynolds to Mrs. Reynolds, wondering if maybe they was pulling my leg some, but they only smiled real bright like they was happy to have just learned something new. I swear, they must've been the only two people in Kennisaw, maybe even the whole hill country, that didn't know a thing about football. And still, here they was, interested in me anyways.

After that, nobody brought up football again, and pretty soon Sara suggested we ought to go on and get to our homework. "I thought we could study in the garage," she said. "My dad had it converted into a library."

I couldn't believe it. I figured a converted garage was every bit as good as a converted basement any day. "That sounds okay," I said, which was pretty much the understatement of my life so far.

"But I forgot." Her eyebrows arched up and I knew I was

in for a letdown. "My sister's book club's meeting in there tonight."

That was more my kind of luck. "Your sister's in a book club?" I said. "I thought she was only about thirteen or fourteen."

"She's twelve. Why?"

"Oh, nothing," I said, but I had to shake my head over that idea. At twelve, you wouldn't have got me to open any book I didn't one hundred percent have to. Matter of fact, I was surprised you could round up enough twelve-year-olds in Kennisaw to fill out a book club.

"I guess we could go over to the library," she suggested. "At least it'll be quiet."

"We could," I said, but the library with its yellow tables and shushing librarians didn't even come close to fitting the mood I was hoping for. "Or maybe we could go down to Sweet's Café and get us a table in the back. I bet there won't hardly be a soul there this late."

"You think?" She cocked her head. "I don't know. I don't think cafés let you hang around doing homework all evening."

"Sure they will. My buddy Jake's parents own it. We hang out there all the time. His sister'll be working tonight. She won't care how long we set in there."

"That sounds great, then." Her face kind of lit up, and she sounded almost like someone accepting a date.

"Great," I said back. I was pretty proud of myself. For once, I'd done come up with a good idea right on the spot instead of thinking of it a day too late. "I hope you don't mind walking. It's only about ten minutes. My mom needed the car tonight."

"I don't mind. It's nice out."

Things was looking like they was working out real good, but just as she was slipping into a light jacket, I realized what I should've realized right from the get-go. What if Jake come sauntering into the café to kill some time? And worse than that, what if Blaine was with him?

Sara had her jacket on. "Ready?"

"You bet," I said. It was too late now. All I could do was hope Jake and Blaine had better things to do tonight.

CHAPTER NINE

Jake's big sister, Sheryl, didn't say nothing. She just stood there a few feet from the table and stared at us.

"What?" I said finally.

"Oh, nothing," she said. "I was just thinking how nice it is to have you in here with your girl instead of Blaine for a change."

I glanced over at Sara to check on how she took the "your girl" remark, but I couldn't tell much with her hair hiding most of her face.

"Don't get me wrong," Sheryl said. "Blaine's okay, but he don't always know when to put all his teasing up and just be hisself. You sure you two don't want a slice of pie to help you study?"

"No, we're okay." I knew Sheryl was only trying to kind of

prod things along between me and Sara, probably thought I couldn't do it for myself, but right now I just wanted to be left alone.

"Well, if y'all need refills on your Cokes, go on back behind the counter and fill your cups up whenever you want." She tossed me a nice, encouraging smile and walked away.

Like I figured, the place was pretty dead, it being a Monday night. The red vinyl-covered chairs was mostly empty, and the little square Formica-topped tables was bare except for their salt and pepper shakers and napkin holders. They had this electric sign buzzing in the window. SWEET'S GOOD EATS! COME ON IN, it said in red lights, but nobody but a couple of old-timers up at the front counter had took them up on the offer tonight.

The bell over the front door jingled and I whipped around, half afraid of seeing Jake and Blaine, but it was only lonesome old Mr. Derryberry shuffling in to take his place up at the counter with the other old bachelors.

"You expecting someone?" Sara asked.

"No, not really," I said.

Across the café, Sheryl cranked up the jukebox, a slow country song, one of the rare ones about love that hadn't gone wrong yet. Pretty obvious she didn't pick that one out for Mr. Derryberry.

I had to admit this place was even better than a converted basement or garage would've been. If I'd got on a couch alone with Sara, I most likely would've started hearing my friends' voices in my head, saying, *Put your arm around her, dumbass. Grab her hand. Kiss her. Reach up under her shirt.* Probably would've been as big a disaster as the time I spilt that chili on Kim Hunt in her white blouse. Here, I could take things slow and easy. Be myself more. As long as Jake and Blaine didn't come strolling in next time that bell over the door went to jingling.

The other big worry I had didn't turn out so bad. This whole time, I was afraid Sara would discover how terrible I really was with textbooks. Not that I had a problem reading. Give me the sports page or something else I'm interested in, and I'd go right to town on it. But studying was a whole different animal. Must have been fourth grade last time Mom or anyone else set down to help me with my homework, and I don't guess my skills had got much better since. If I had a list of terms or names or something like that to look up, everything just seemed to turn into Egyptian hieroglyphics right in front of my eyes. In the study group, I figured Sara just thought I was slower finding the answers than everyone else, but here, one-on-one, she was bound to find out what kind of a real idiot I was.

A funny thing happened, though, when we got to working on the assignment. Sara showed me how to pick out the most important words or names from out of the worksheet questions and look them up in the index of the book. I hate to admit it, but I didn't even know the book had an index! I'd always scraped by without reading that far back. But just that one little tip was the difference between sinking and swimming right there. I started finding answers so quick, I got to wondering if maybe I wasn't dumb after all. I might even be a little bit smart in my own way.

By the time we got down towards the last few questions, I was starting to feel kind of like a Civil War expert. If Darnell and Lana Pitt wanted my opinion on the Confederacy now, I was ready. It even crossed my mind that I might order off one of them Civil War chess sets they show on TV, hang around out in Sara's converted-garage library learning how to play it with her.

"Did you find the one about Matthew Brady yet?" she asked.

"Page two thirty-four," I said.

She looked up from her paper. "You're really good at this. How come you don't say that much when we're in our study group?"

"Well, to tell you the truth, I wasn't good at it till you told me I oughta look things up in the index. I'd just set around turning pages, hoping an answer would jump up and bite me, I guess." It's funny how you can be honest about things like that once you stop worrying about them.

She laughed. "You weren't that bad."

"No, really," I said. "You oughta be a teacher."

"Thanks." She looked down in her shy way and smiled, and I thought that'd be hard to beat right there, making her smile like that.

Conversation was smooth sailing after that. She talked about living over in Oklahoma City before moving here, and I told a little about living up in Poynter. We had a good time trading stories about what we was like as little kids, the friends we'd had and left behind when we moved, what kind of games we played, the Halloween costumes we wore, and what kind of trick-or-treat candy was our favorite. All sorts of things. It wasn't nothing like what my buddies told me about them and their girls.

Talking about the days back in Poynter, I skipped over the serious part—the old sad story about my dad running off—but Sara, she didn't skip over nothing. They had a tough time back where she used to live after her dad's accident, almost tore the family apart, she said, but now they was stronger for getting through it.

"How'd it happen?" I asked. "The accident."

"Drunk driver. Seven years ago. Dad had a flat tire on the interstate and pulled over on the shoulder. He'd just shut off the engine when this drunk girl—I think she was only about twenty-two or twenty-three—plowed into the back of his car and spun it back out into traffic. A semi hit him then, flipped his little Honda right over the guardrail. He was lucky to be alive. That's how he looked at it right from the start. The rest of us didn't deal with it half as well as he did. Especially me. I was just pure trouble there for a while."

"You? That's kind of hard to picture."

"Well, I don't mean I joined a motorcycle gang or anything. I was just ten. But I wasn't doing my homework, and I was always fighting with my sister and my mom and my teachers. Never my dad but everyone else. I basically hated everything. The sidewalk, the mailbox. Set a glass of milk down in front of me, and I hated that."

"What happened? I mean, you sure ain't like that now."

Her eyebrows slanted up, like maybe she thought she could still be that way a little sometimes. "Well, but every once in a while, when I see my dad struggling with something simple like putting his shoes on, it still makes me mad."

"I don't blame you." I was starting to see how she got that sad-for-the-world look in her eyes.

"I guess the turning point for me came one day when I was with my dad at the hospital. There were all these doctors in white coats walking by like ghosts, and the rooms filled up with people who'd gone wrong in some way, and it just hit me. Maybe I should try to do something to make them right again. And to be honest, I think I was so mad about what happened, at how unfair it seemed, that I figured if I helped fix people it would be like getting even with whatever hurt my dad. Sort of like getting revenge, almost. That's when I made up my mind to go to medical school. From then on, I always felt like I was doing something about what happened, making something out of it."

"Wow," I said.

"I didn't mean to get so serious like that."

"No," I said. "I'm glad you told me." I studied the salt-shaker for a moment. I knew I had to tell her about my dad after all. It would've been selfish somehow if I didn't after what all she just told me. "My dad run off on us," I said, just like that. "I don't even see him anymore."

"How old were you?"

"Eight. I guess it was like its own kind of car wreck in a way. My mom sure didn't come out the same afterwards. But I don't guess either one of us had one of them hospital moments when we realized what to do about it."

I could feel her looking at me, but I couldn't do nothing but stare an extra set of holes in that saltshaker. I was afraid if I looked up in them brown eyes right then, I might have to realize who I really was after all, and I didn't think I was ready for that.

"I'm sure you'll figure it out one of these days," she said.

"Maybe."

"Have you thought about what you're going to do after high school?"

I knew what she was doing—trying to get the conversation back on something lighter. It was one more thing to like her for.

"I'll play college ball," I said, shifting in my seat. "See how that goes. If pros don't work out after that, I guess I'll go into coaching. I don't know what kind of coach I'd make—I ain't that great at telling folks what to do—but that's pretty much the only other thing there is if you don't go pro."

"There's other things besides sports," she suggested.

"I know, but I ain't much good at anything else. Blaine's dad told us if we want to succeed at something, we have to set our sights on that one thing and go after it, and for me that one thing is pretty much football."

"You don't have to do it just because he said so, you know. You could experiment around, maybe find something else too."

"Uh, yeah, I guess I don't *have* to." She'd caught me off guard with that. I mean, Blaine and his dad was pretty much the only ones outside of my coaches that ever bothered to give me much in the way of advice. Didn't hardly seem right for Sara to jump in and start questioning an authority like Mr. Keller.

"I'm just saying, it's your life," she said.

"I know." I was back to staring down the saltshaker. All the sudden, it was real important to make Sara understand how it was with me and the Kellers, but I didn't know how to go about it. Her father might've been in a wheelchair, but at least he was there. All I had was Blaine and his dad.

"It's not that there's anything wrong with football," she said. "But you surely have some other interests too."

"Well." I was starting to feel unsure of myself again. "I like to go hunting."

"Hunting?"

I realized how stupid that sounded. Like maybe I thought I'd make me a career out of hunting later on, wearing a safari jacket and one of them funny-looking round helmets and all.

The whole conversation had been going so good, and now it was coming apart faster than the Lowery Mud Hens' defensive line.

"I mean, it's not so much the hunting part I like." I was stumbling around the way I do when I haven't thought things through. "My real favorite part of it is just being out there in the woods. You get out there early in the morning with the dew still on the leaves and the grass and everything, and it's just a whole different world. The sun's coming up, and it's cool and quiet, and everything's real still. It's like you're part of everything around, and you just get this huge feeling inside. That's what I like."

I looked up, expecting her to be staring at me like I was a crazy man, but she wasn't.

"Sounds nice," she said. She was looking off towards the wall like she could see the morning sun hanging over the hill instead of the antique Coke signs and wagon wheels that really hung up there.

"You don't think it sounds stupid?"

"No. Why would I think that?"

"Oh, you know, the big jock talking about walking around in nature, looking at the sun coming up and all."

"You know what I think?" she said. "I think you sound real spiritual."

"Spiritual? Me? I don't know about that. The only times I get to church is when the Kellers take me with them. My mom stopped going a long time ago."

"I don't mean it like that. Not spiritual like a preacher or anything. It's just how you are inside. You're quiet but not so much in a shy way. More like you're waiting till there's something worthwhile to say."

I had to laugh at that. "I guess I haven't found it yet."

"Oh, I don't know." She twisted a wild strand of hair around her finger for a second. "Maybe you just haven't found the right person to hear it yet. What you were just saying about walking out in the woods in the morning, that sounded pretty worthwhile to me."

"I sure like it out there," I said, feeling like I'd somehow got the conversation back on the right track. "You should go check it out sometime. There's a great place to go right out on the other side of Highway Two."

She looked down, and her hair hid most of her face. "I will."

That's when it hit me. *You stupid idiot, you need to tell this girl that you'll take her out there your own self.* It was as clear as day. I could take her out there this weekend, go to all the best spots, bring some sandwiches, hike up to them cliffs over Lake Hawkshaw, and look off across the water to where the hills rolled away into the sky.

The bell over the door jingled.

Before I even got turned all the way around, I knew who come in. It was just my luck with girls. There they was, Jake and Blaine.

"Hey, Sheryl," Jake called to his sister. "Set us up some Cokes."

"Get 'em yourself," she told him.

"Aw now, Sheryl," Blaine said. "Is that any way to act towards a couple hardworking football players?"

I could wish all I wanted that they'd just hang around at the front counter and not pay any attention to us in the back, but it wouldn't do no good.

"What the hell?" Blaine grinned real big when he seen me, but it wasn't a friendly grin. "I can't believe my eyes. It's the great Hampton Green. Who's this here you're with, Hamp, your personal secretary?"

"Hey now," Sheryl said. "You leave them alone and come get you a Coke."

Course, it didn't do no good. Jake and Blaine headed straight for our table.

"Don't tell me you're in here doing actual homework," Jake said, eyeing over the textbooks setting there on the table.

"Hampton doing homework? No way." Blaine pulled out a chair, spun it around, and set down with his arms resting on the back of it. "I don't believe we've met," he said to Sara, like he didn't even know who she was. "I'm Blaine Keller."

"I know," she said. "We've been going to the same school since eighth grade."

"So, what's the deal? You filling my boy in on all the answers?" Blaine picked up her history book and pretended to look it over.

"Actually," she said, "Hampton's been finding most of the answers."

"No way," Jake said.

I started to come out with how interesting some of that Civil War stuff was, but I knew neither one of them boys would buy that. Probably would've thought I was trying to put on a show for Sara. Fact was, I couldn't hardly think up anything decent to say. It was almost like I was setting between two sides of people who didn't speak the same language.

"How'd y'all get here anyways?" Blaine set the book down. "You walk?"

"Yeah," I said, looking down.

"Damn, son, you must've been desperate to get some help. That's a good thirty-minute hike for you."

"Really?" Sara said. "I didn't know you had to walk that far to my house."

I shrugged.

"I'll get my mom to drive you home when we get back," she said.

"Naw, forget that," Blaine said. "I'll drive y'all home."

I glared at him. "That's okay."

"Are you kidding? It's no problem." He gave me the wide-eyed innocent look, but he knew it was a problem, all right. For me. "Just let me and Jake throw back a couple Cokes real quick. We can't have Kennisaw's star linebacker traipsing all over town after football practice. You might blow out an ankle or something."

This would've been a perfect moment for my time-freezing skill to kick in, but there wasn't no chance for it to work when it come to dealing with people like this. I couldn't think of excuse one. The café was closing and the Civil War worksheet was about all filled out. Nothing left to do but just go along.

Blaine and Jake got their Cokes, and me and Sara packed our books into our backpacks. Citronella was parked out front, one tire up on the curb. I climbed into the back along with Sara, but I doubted there'd be much chance between here and her house to talk to her about any walks in the country or anything else.

We hadn't no more than pulled away from the curb when Blaine started in. "Hey, Sara, did Hamp tell you how I saved his life back in junior high?" He glanced at her in the rearview mirror. "Really, I saved his life more than once, but this one time back in seventh grade when he got involved with square dancing, he would've been toast if I hadn't come along."

"Not that story," I groaned.

"The deal was, his mother started dating this nerdy little guy who was some kind of kingpin in square-dancing clubs, so she joined up and made Hampton get in the junior square-dancing league or whatever it was called. It was hilarious. He shows up outside the junior high gym for some kind of practice or competition or something, and he's wearing this whole outfit. Red straw hat, red shirt and neckerchief, and red pants. Red damn pants!"

Jake laughed. "Hampton Green, the dancing machine!"

You can bet I was blushing redder than any square-dancing outfit ever thought about being. I glanced over at Sara but couldn't read her expression. I hoped maybe she wouldn't think red pants and a red straw hat was as stupid as everyone else. Or at least that she'd figure I wasn't real likely to dress that way if we was ever to go for a walk in the country together.

"Well," Blaine went on, shooting Sara another look in the rearview mirror. "You can probably guess what happened. Hamp's waiting around out in the parking lot there, and these five eighth graders come up, and they can't believe their eyes. They swoop right in on him like a pack of blue jays and start calling him cowgirl and Dolly Parton and all kinds of names. And one guy gets to shoving him, saying, 'Come on, Dolly, get out your guitar and sing us a song.'

"That's when I rode up on my bike. Now, Hamp and me have been buddies since fourth grade, so I ain't gonna set still for this kind of stuff out of a few measly eighth graders. So I charge right up into the middle of 'em and say, 'All right there, tough guys, just back on off if you don't want to have to drag your butts out of here in a sling.'"

"That's not exactly how I remember it," I said, but old Blaine just kept going without missing a beat.

"Then the biggest one of 'em asks me where my army is, 'cause I'm gonna need one in about two seconds. Usually, I would've pitched in right then and started swinging, but there was five of these dudes. And they was *big*! So I had to think fast. So I said, 'Boys, boys, we ain't got time to fight. Can't you see my buddy here has a date with ten different girls at the same time?'

"That sure got their attention. They all wanted to know how one kid, and a seventh grader to boot, could get a date with ten different girls. So I went into this whole deal about how these square-dancing clubs was almost completely made up of girls, and any time they could get a real live boy to dance with instead of another girl, they was all over him like shark bait.

"Course, old Hamp didn't even know which end was up on a girl, but I had them boys convinced he was a one-man wrecking crew. By the time I got done, every one of 'em was ready to go out and buy their own pair of red pants and get to do-si-do-ing all over the place. But I'll guarantee you I got Hamp out of there, and he ain't never square-danced another lick since then."

I checked Sara again to see how disgusted she was with me, but she just stared straight into the rearview mirror at Blaine and said, "There isn't anything wrong with square dancing."

It took Blaine a little off guard 'cause he couldn't even get one of his usual snickery comebacks fired off before old Jake cut in with a story of his own.

"Hey," he said. "Have y'all ever heard the one about the three cheerleaders and the giant pickle?"

I was pretty relieved there. It was fixing to be one of Jake's dirty jokes, but that was still a far sight better than Blaine telling any more of his tales. I just wanted to get back to Sara's house, maybe walk her up to the door and talk to her in private for a second at least.

Jake's story was just winding down when we got there. He turned around to deliver the last line. "And the third cheerleader says, 'That's not a pickle!'"

Nobody but him and Blaine laughed. Sara just shot me this kind of painful smile and reached over for the door handle. She looked about like she was ready to jump out the door before we even stopped all the way. Before I could say anything, she done looped the strap of her backpack over her shoulder and was standing on the driveway looking back in at me. I never even got a chance to offer to walk her to the door.

"I'll see you at school tomorrow," she said.

"Yeah," I said. "I'll see you there. I'll look up them last two answers on the worksheet when I get home."

She started to close the door but then stopped, and a nervous little flicker showed up in her eyes. "I was wondering," she said. "My parents told me there's going to be a real good bluegrass band playing over at the Wild West Days festival this weekend. Have you heard about that?"

"No," I said, not picking up on a single clue of what she was hinting at. "I don't know much about bluegrass music."

"So, I guess you hadn't thought about going over there, then?"

"I hadn't thought about it, no." Then it dawned on me. What an idiot I was. She wanted to go see that band. But before I could say I thought it sounded like fun, Blaine cut right in on me.

"Sure, you thought about it," he said, looking back at me. "Remember, Rachel and me and you and Misty are going over there together. It's all set."

All I could get out then was, "Uh, well . . ."

Sara ducked her head and her hair blew across her face. "Okay, maybe I'll see you there, then." Next thing you know the door was shut and she was halfway up the sidewalk.

Blaine laughed and shoved the shifter into gear. "Yeah, I could just see you taking Bush Girl to Wild West Days."

"Don't call her that," I said, but that only got him laughing louder.

CHAPTER TEN

Next football practice was pretty intense. Friday's game was only against the little old Pawtuska Pirates, but Coach let us know loud and clear we didn't have no room for letup unless we wanted to fumble away our one and only chance at a fifth straight undefeated season. I didn't think he should've used the word *fumble* like that, sort of hinting back to how Blaine fumbled against Wynette. That was uncalled-for. But if he was trying to get Blaine motivated, it sure worked.

That whole practice long, any time Blaine got the ball, he just wouldn't go down. Running up the middle, he never broke loose for much yardage, but even when the whole defensive line stood him up straight and plowed him backwards into the backfield, he'd just keep swinging his elbows and kicking his legs up till the whistle blew.

Every snap, he went looking for someone to hit whuther he had the ball or not. One time he clocked little Tommy Nguyen so hard, Tommy flew backwards about five yards and come down headfirst into the ground about like a tent spike. He smashed up into that oversize helmet of his so far, I thought they was going to have to find a crowbar to pry him out of there. But that was Blaine. He wanted them five unde-feated seasons worse than anyone else.

I know his knee had to be killing him too. Instead of let-ting one of the assistant coaches wrap it before practice, he done it hisself so nobody could see how much it'd swole up again after that last big hit he took against Wynette. But when he got on the field, he gave it everything he had. I just admired the soup out of him for the way he went at it that day—sweat and blood and fists all flying.

It wasn't till after practice that I found out how he lied to me.

We got our showers in, then me and him loaded up in Citronella and headed over to Rachel's house to talk over the details of our double date on Saturday night. Rachel lived up on Ninth Street Hill in this big old white-brick two-story house with a wide front porch and a giant flower bed that they hired someone else to take care of. I waited in the car while Blaine went up to the door. Standing there on that porch in his backwards ball cap and wore-out Dallas Cowboys sweatshirt, he looked about like he could've been the hired help his own self.

Blaine wasn't poor, not by a long shot. His dad was a shift supervisor over at the glass plant, and their house was sure a lot nicer than the little rent house me and my mom smooshed ourselves into. It might not have been anywheres near big as Rachel's, but Mr. Keller kept the white board walls with the green trim, the lawn, and all the shrubs about as neat as a marine sergeant's bunk bed on inspection day. He was a pure nut for lawn equipment—the louder the better.

On the other hand, Rachel's dad owned hisself the big furniture store on the edge of town, along with one in Lowery and another one he was just getting started in Wynette. She always had the best of everything—new clothes, a horse with its own pink trailer, a brand-spanking-new Dodge Durango SUV. None of that bothered Blaine. That was just the kind of girl he was *supposed* to have, he always said. He was as sure of that as he was of how our football team was fixing to go down in history alongside old T. Roy Strong's team of thirty years ago.

Rachel's mom poked her head out and talked to Blaine for a second or two and then shut the door. He walked off the front porch, slamming the post there with the flat of his hand on his way.

"What's the matter?" I asked when he got in the car. "Ain't there?"

"Naw, she's down at the furniture store. And I told her clear as day what time I was coming over here." Blaine stuck the shifter in gear and we headed back down Ninth Street. "That girl's starting to wear me out a little. Getting a lip on her too. Tell you what, if she wasn't so good-looking, I might switch over to Misty Koonce myself."

"You don't mean that. You been with Rachel almost two years."

He grinned. "Don't worry, Hamp. I ain't gonna steal Misty from you."

"I ain't worried." I looked out the side window. "Go ahead and steal her if you want to."

"That Misty, she's a hot one." He let out a high whistle.

71

"Fact is, I don't know how crazy Rachel's gonna be about getting Misty to come along on one of our dates, but it'll do her some good to get a little jealous for a change."

That's when it hit me that Blaine'd lied. "Wait a minute," I said. "Rachel don't know about it yet? I thought you said everything was already set up."

"It is." He fiddled with the radio buttons for a second, tuning in a country station. "I mean, maybe I ain't actually talked to Rachel about fixing you two up yet, but that's all right. I got that girl in my hip pocket. Besides, how's she gonna say no with you standing right there?"

"Hey, I never even said I wanted to do this in the first place. I ain't got the first idea what I'd say to Misty Koonce on a date."

He took his eyes off the road to size me up. "You ain't still thinking about that Bush Girl, are you?"

I looked away out the window again. "Her name's Sara."

He gave the steering wheel a little slap. "I knew it. You got a thing for her."

"I don't know if you'd call it a *thing*. All I know is we can set there and talk and it's just about like no time's gone by at all."

"So what? I hope you don't think that means you got some kind of *deep connection* or something, 'cause that's bull. Let me ask you this. How much does she know about football?"

"Not too much."

"See there. If she don't understand football, she don't understand you."

I had to admit Blaine had a point there. She probably didn't have the least idea how football pretty much saved me when I moved to Kennisaw after my dad run off.

"I'm just trying to do you a favor," Blaine went on.

" 'Cause if you think you're gonna change her, you can forget that. You don't change them, man, they change you. Look at what happened to my brother and that train wreck he got married to."

"That was different," I said. "Billy married a crystal-meth freak."

"That ain't the point." Blaine was getting irritated. "The point is he changed. I don't even know where he's living now—somewheres on the north side of Tulsa, I think, but nobody knows his address. My parents don't even talk to him no more. Don't even mention his name."

"That's messed up," I said. "He's still family."

Blaine stared a cold hole in the windshield. "No he's not."

He looked like he really meant it too. The family could just lop old Billy off like a rotten branch. He wasn't really such a bad guy neither, just different from the rest of the Kellers. Quit football before high school, always talked about things like hitchhiking around the country or taking a steamboat to Malaysia, going to chef school, starting up a country-rock band. Me, I liked Billy, but him and Mr. Keller was always butting heads, and Blaine kind of gave up on him when he dropped football.

But I guessed cutting Billy off was about the same as the way my dad cut me and my mom off. It's a hard way to go, knowing your family can split up at the drop of a hat like that. I thought back to how Blaine played in practice today, and it dawned on me that maybe Coach Huff wasn't the biggest thing motivating him after all.

"What I'm saying is this." Blaine was still staring hard through the windshield. "I don't want to lose my best friend the same way I lost my brother."

"That ain't gonna happen," I said. I still wasn't convinced

on the Misty-against-Sara deal, but there wasn't much else to say. Me and Blaine had been good buddies for a long time, but he'd never compared me to his brother right out loud like that before.

At the furniture store, Blaine slung open the front door, strolled in, and surveyed over them rows of sofas and easy chairs about like he was the heir of a big Southern plantation, just taking a good look at what all he was fixing to inherit. He picked up a floweredy pillow, lateraled it back to me, and said, "Throw me a long bomb, Hamp."

When he took off down the aisle, I heaved the pillow end over end, leading him just a whisker too much. He had to make a diving catch and landed hard on this blue crushed-velvet sofa with an eight-hundred-dollar price tag on the arm. It let out a little whimpering moan that didn't exactly sound healthy.

Una Lewis, the salesclerk, come shuffling down the aisle from the back of the store. "You boys tear anything up out here and you buy it." Una looked like she could've been a hundred years old and had worked for Calloway Furniture ever since Rachel's granddad started the business back in the old building on Main.

"Aw now, Una," Blaine said. "You know your furniture's too high quality for a dainty little thing like me to hurt it." He stood up and tossed the pillow down on the sofa. "Where's Rachel—in the back talking to her dad?"

"Her daddy's not here," Una said in that usual abrupt way she had. "He's over at the Wynette store."

Blaine said he seen the Durango parked out front so he figured Rachel had to be around somewheres, and Una said, "I didn't say she wasn't here. I said her daddy wasn't. She's in the back office talking to Don."

"Uh-oh," I said. "Rachel's getting a little flirting time in with big Don." I was just kidding—Don Manly wasn't any kind of big, and I never thought for a second Rachel was back there flirting with him. But Blaine shot me this real dirty look and headed off for the back so fast you'd have thought he was on a mission. I had to double-step just to catch up with him.

The office was located at the end of the storeroom, and as we got up close, you could hear Rachel's voice. Blaine stopped right beside the door and waved for me to stand next to him. He craned his head so he could hear her better.

"I'll tell you this for sure," she said. "I know I don't want to end up hanging around this sorry town forever. I might not even want to stay in this state." There was something strange about her voice, kind of like she was looking to finagle Don's stamp of approval or something. That was different. Most of the time, she acted like she didn't give a powdered donut hole what anybody else thought.

Don come back with some advice. "What I do is list goals down in writing, and then every day I look at that list and ask myself what I have to do to get there." He was trying to sound official about it, like one of them authorities they get on daytime talk shows to tell folks why it ain't a good idea to sleep with their sisters.

Don hadn't been much in high school, hadn't even played football, but he went up to Tulsa and got hisself an associate's degree in business from the junior college, and he thought he was a hotshot now. Mr. Calloway even made him full store manager for the Kennisaw location. But I figured, so what?

Maybe some of the girls said he was good-looking, but you couldn't prove it by me.

Old Blaine, though—he looked about like he done swallowed a box of nails. It sure wasn't the kind of look you expect from a guy who thinks he has his girl in his hip pocket.

"If I was gonna have a list," Rachel said, "first thing I'd put on there is that I want to live in a place where you can go to a good department store any time you want instead of just Wal-Mart. And I want a house with exactly twelve rooms. Maybe one of those ones with the big white columns out front."

"Plantation-style," Don said. You could smell his cologne, stronger than gasoline, all the way out where we was standing. "Columns like that date back to ancient Greek architecture."

Blaine looked at me and rolled his eyes.

"Or I might want me a colonial type," Rachel said. "White with green shutters."

"Like in Vermont."

"Only I'd have mine down in Dallas, and I'd have a circle driveway with a fountain in the middle of it and a swimming pool shaped like a star in the backyard."

"Dallas would be fantastic," Don said. "That's where I'm gonna start up my real estate business. I've got me a book on how you can retire at thirty years old off nothing but real estate investments alone."

Right about there was when I noticed Blaine's ears had done went red and he was twisting at the tail of his sweatshirt so hard you would've thought he was practicing up on how to wring old Don's neck. Now, what they was saying might seem pretty tame, but you got to understand Blaine.

No doubt he was figuring it ought to be him talking to Rachel about living in Dallas, not Don Manly. Blaine'd dreamed of moving there ever since we was kids. He aimed on playing pro ball for the Cowboys just like T. Roy Strong and living in one of them big mirror-window high-rises and driving a red Lamborghini all over town. Now we just had us a handful of games left to prove we was worth moving on to college ball, much less the pros. Time was running out. You could practically feel it, like blood running out of a nasty wound.

"Hey, it's getting late," Don said. "I better go lock up."

Right quick, Blaine leaned away from the wall and pretended like he was just now getting to the door. Rachel almost crashed into him as she walked out ahead of Don.

"Whoa there," Blaine said, grabbing her arm like he was surprised to run into her. "Watch where you're going." Then he looked over her head. "Hey, Donnyboy, how's business?"

Don squeezed by. "Fantastic. How you doing, Billy?"

"It's Blaine."

Don didn't pay the least attention to that and just kept on walking, that high-octane cologne smell trailing right along after him.

"What a dick," Blaine muttered under his breath.

"So, what are you doing here?" Rachel said. Her voice had got its old edge back.

"I just stopped by to see my girlfriend." Blaine stood there with his hands planted on his hips gunfighter-style. "But what I want to know is why my girlfriend was in there flirting with Don Manly."

"*Flirting?*" She put her hands on her hips too. You'd have thought it was the OK Corral all the sudden.

"You know what I mean," he said. "Talking all about how the two of you are gonna live in Dallas together."

Her mouth froze into a little O for a moment before she shot back at him. "We weren't talking about living down there *together*. And what were you doing anyways, standing out here spying on us?"

That one hit Blaine right on target. He leaned back against the wall. "Yeah, right. That's my new hobby. No, for your information, little girl, I didn't have to do no spying. You was talking loud enough Una could probably hear you out in the showroom, and you know how deaf she is."

"Una ain't deaf—she's just old."

"Well, don't get snippy. What's the deal? You mad 'cause you didn't get a chance to tell Don how you was gonna fix up your fancy bedroom in your big twelve-room mansion? Or you planning on showing it to him in person someday?"

"What's that supposed to mean?" She leaned in close enough it wouldn't have been hard for her to take a swing from there. You couldn't blame her if she did, with him saying something like that.

"What do you think it's supposed to mean?" he said. "Sounded to me like you and Donnyboy was getting pretty personal in there."

She stepped back and looked Blaine up and down. "So, this is what Blaine Keller looks like jealous, huh?"

"Jealous?" He crossed his arms and looked away. "That'll be the day, when I'm jealous of a pansy like Don Manly."

But she was right. I didn't know what the world was coming to anymore. Cocky old Blaine was worried—down-to-the-soles-of-his-boots worried—about his girl throwing him over for Don Manly. Don damn Manly with his flashy neckties and gelled-up hair and that phony zirconium ring on his pinky. Blaine was jealous, his brother was kicked out of the family, and his cantaloupe-size knee was dragging down his senior football season. None of that seemed any more like the Blaine I knew than if you told me he tried out for drum majorette or glee club or bought hisself one of them little electric cars.

"You are," Rachel said. "You're jealous."

"You're crazy."

"Yes, you are. Blainey's jealous." Her voice was different now. Playful in a hard, roughhousing kind of way. "Check him out, Hampton," she said. "He's just about turned green as a lizard, don't you think?"

"I don't know," I said.

"Just a big old green jealous lizard," she said, and dug her knuckles into his ribs.

He squirmed away, but she dug into him again, tickling him and teasing him, till that hard line he tried to keep his mouth froze in melted into a little smile. I was glad to see it. I liked Rachel. She was good for Blaine—always told him right off what she thought—and I didn't no more want them to break up than I wanted to lose Blaine as a friend myself.

"You're asking for it," he said, but he was just right on the edge of laughing now, and the wrong stretch was over. "You better stop or I'm gonna let you have it."

She dug into him again, and he looped one arm around her neck and pressed her head to his chest. "You gonna stop?" he said.

She stomped down right in the middle of his boot then, and he wrenched away. "Holy shit!"

"That'll teach you," she told him, laughing.

But his face screwed up with pain, and he leaned back into the wall and cocked his leg up like she really hurt him.

"What's the matter?" she said. "I didn't stomp on your big old foot that hard."

"I know. It's okay." He straightened his leg out, wincing again. "Just twisted my knee a little when I pulled away."

"God, I'm sorry." She touched her hand to his stomach, gentle this time. "Is your knee that bad off?"

"No. It's all right. Just tender from practice today is all."

"You want me to make it up to you?" she said.

"What do you got in mind?"

She gave him a playful little slap on the arm. "Probably not what *you* got in mind."

"Now wait a minute," he said. "You got me all wrong."

"Oh, sure. I'd recognize that look in your eye any day."

"No, really. I don't want a thing for myself." He looked at me and winked. I completely forgot till now that we come over to talk about the deal with Misty Koonce.

"I was just thinking," he went on. "You know how Misty just got done dumping that guy with the hot truck over in Lowery? Well, she's single now, and old Hamp here's single, so I was just kind of thinking . . ."

"Sure," she said.

"What?"

"I'll do it. I'll give Misty a call tonight."

So that was that. I never even had a chance to say word one about it.

Blaine looked over Rachel's head and smiled his cocky smile. "See, Hamp," he said. "Told ya I got this girl in my hip pocket."

CHAPTER ELEVEN

By the time Friday come around, we was plenty prepared for the little old Pawtuska Pirates. It was our last away game of the regular season and almost an hour's drive from home, but our loyal Kennisaw fans still come over in such a herd they overflowed the flimsy visitor bleachers and crowded onto the Pirate side. Blaine's folks set front and center like usual and Rachel set next to them and then there was Misty right by her. You might've thought Rachel and Misty would be cheerleaders, flipping end over end down the sideline, but neither one of them was really the flipping type.

One thing I learned is the most popular good-looking girls don't always care a thing about being the head cheerleader. As long as their folks got plenty of money. Sure, they run in the same circle with the cheerleaders, but it's almost like the

81

cheerleaders are their employees somehow. Like they hired them on to work up a good amount of attention for their group so they don't have to break a sweat their own selves.

It was good to see Rachel's face painted up black and gold, though. That wasn't exactly typical for her, but she must've figured Blaine needed a little extra support these days. Misty, well, I checked her out now and then from the sidelines, but every time, she was craning her head one way or the other, gawking up in the stands instead of looking down on the field. Rachel said she gave it the okay for the double date on Saturday, but she sure didn't seem too interested in what I was doing tonight.

From the first quarter, the game wasn't no contest. Pawtuska couldn't make no more headway against our defense than you could trying to hammer a rubber nail into a concrete wall. I got in a fair amount of tackles, but our line played great too. Still, early on, the Kennisaw fans got to chanting my name just like in the last game, even when I didn't do nothing but help out on a tackle that somebody else got started. I wouldn't have blamed the boys on the line if they got put out about it, but they never said a thing. Old Blaine sure did, though.

"What are you doing?" he yelled at me as I run off the field with the chants raining down on me.

"What are you talking about?" I said.

He latched up his chin strap, getting ready to go in on offense. "You got the whole crowd hollering your name when you wasn't even the one got the tackle!"

"I didn't tell 'em to," I said, pulling my helmet off.

"Well, it ain't right."

I wanted to ask him what he expected me to do about it,

but he was already running onto the field. Didn't matter anyways. We was getting so far ahead, Coach was bound to pull me out of the lineup pretty soon and let the second string play. Besides, I knew Blaine was just frustrated. Wasn't nothing that a good game wouldn't cure. That's what I was rooting for more than about anything else—just for Blaine to put up some big numbers, remind our fans what kind of football player he really was.

By the end of the first half, he done got a real fine start in that direction too. We scored thirty-two points, and Blaine hung three of them touchdowns up on the scoreboard hisself. On the third one, the crowd about went crazy, and someone got the chant going, "Undefeated, undefeated, undefeated!" Blaine run off the field, shoving his hands up in the air, telling them to turn up the noise as loud as they could go. It was good to see. So far, his touchdown runs hadn't been nothing more than three- or four-yard blasts up the middle, but that didn't matter. Blaine was just a natural star, and he deserved every cheer he got.

Through most of the third quarter, it was the same story. He pounded out short gainers and kept us in first downs, but you had to know he wanted more. Something spectacular. A run folks would still be talking about come Monday. Or better than that, the kind of big play they'd still be telling tales about thirty years down the line, the way they did on T. Roy Strong. But that wasn't going to be easy with his knee the way it was. Every time he tried a quick cut or a stutter step or anything like that, I could just feel the pain of it shooting through my own gut.

By the end of the quarter, most of our bench was out on the field, but Coach kept Blaine in the game. He knew every bit as much as I did what old Blaine had at stake. Then it finally happened. Second down and five, Chili Killiebrew drove his man clean back on his butt, and Blaine charged through the opening quicker than I'd seen him do all year. He made a good cut and lost the middle linebacker, then bounced off the outside linebacker and turned upfield. Ten yards, fifteen, twenty. Nothing but open field ahead. The crowd was going wild. Racing down the sideline, Blaine looked free, the way a good horse looks when it's running just to run.

Then I seen him, number twenty-two, the right cornerback, galloping after Blaine at a hard angle, knees pumping, hands slicing the air. That boy was fast, and you could tell he didn't have no sore knee to deal with neither.

"Turn it on, Blaine!" I yelled. "Turn the jets on, son! Let's go!"

But there wasn't no jets to turn on this season. He couldn't even find the switch, and before you knew it, that cornerback caught him and dragged him down like so much rodeo livestock. It was a good forty-yarder, and the crowd howled and howled like it wasn't never going to stop, but I knew the same thing Blaine did. He ought to still be running. He ought to be high-stepping right across the goal line, that cornerback trailing way behind with nothing to catch but his breath.

Five plays later, Blaine bucked his way in for another touchdown. A one-yarder. The score was 48 to 0. I know them poor old Pawtuska boys must've been feeling like roadkill right about then. By the time the fourth quarter rolled around, we had our whole bench cleared off. Even little Grub Sweeney got to go in. When the final gun fired, we ended up winning 57 to 0, one of the most lopsided victories in Kennisaw football history, including the T. Roy days.

After the game, we had all sorts of fans flooding down to slap our backs and tell us we was number one and heading for the history books. Course, Blaine's parents come down and Rachel too. I didn't see Misty nowhere, but Rachel run up with her face painted gold and black like it was and just about knocked Blaine over jumping up on him. She threw her arms around his neck and kissed him a big one right on the mouth. "You were great," she said when he let her back down. "You were fantastic!"

"You're damn right," he said. "I'm back. One hundred and forty-four percent!"

"Yeah, you are," I said, clapping him on the shoulder. "You're the old Blaine again!"

But I guess we both knew that wasn't true.

CHAPTER TWELVE

Saturday night, I put on my best new Wranglers and my black-and-white "Mo" Betta western shirt. Blaine come by about 7:30, and we loaded up in Citronella, along with Rachel, and drove over to pick up Misty Koonce for the big double date. Misty lived up on Ninth Street Hill, just like Rachel, and her house was about as big as Rachel's too. Her dad worked for the natural-gas company, but I ain't sure exactly what he done. Must've been pretty high up, though.

Misty's mom showed up at the front door and made me come inside and say hello to Mr. Koonce. He was older than most of the other dads, probably in his late fifties or so, and had him kind of a phony smile. It could've been 'cause he had false teeth, but I wasn't sure about that. He asked me a couple football questions, but he done it in a way that made me feel like I worked for him and was having to report on what kind of progress I'd been making on some assignment he gave me. Lucky thing Misty come waltzing down the stairs around then 'cause I was feeling like I was about two questions short of getting fired off the job.

She cut right in on what her dad was saying, rattling on in that trademark mile-a-minute way of hers. Without so much as a howdy-do, she grabbed my arm and we was out the door before her dad could finish telling me what time I better have her back by. There wasn't any two ways about it. That girl looked good, all blond-haired and pink-sweatered and perfumed up to high heaven. Rockies jeans and red cowgirl boots. The color of her skin close up was enough to throw my hormones into an uproar all by itself.

It wasn't love. I knew that. But there wasn't no getting around the power of whatever it was that hit me right then neither. I just wondered what a girl like her was doing going out with me.

Like everybody else around, I knew Misty was prejudiced when it come to boys. By the time she traded junior high in for high school, she'd done run through a good-size range of Kennisaw boyfriends, so I guess she decided to go off shopping somewheres else for a fresher selection. As far as I knew, she hadn't dated a Kennisaw boy since she turned old enough to drive. Last target she set her sights on was a kid named Jared Tull from over in Lowery, the same town old Jim Houck the hotshot playboy come from. She hit Jared right between the eyes too.

He wasn't famous for playing football but for owning the fastest pickup truck in two counties. He also had him a reputation, leastways with some of the high school girls, for wearing the tightest black Wrangler jeans that any human being from the planet Earth could fit into without cutting off the blood supply to his legs. You wouldn't hear a girl talking about this character without saying something like, "Oh my God, he has the cutest butt I ever seen!" It was a saying you could get tired of real quick.

I guess about the only thing tighter than them jeans was his relationship with Misty these last three months. That's what everybody thought, anyways. But then somewheres out on a blacktop road west of Lowery, the fastest pickup truck in two counties blew its engine trying to outrun Fred Buck in his little old jacked-up Mustang. He blew up his engine and Misty blew *him* up. That's what Blaine said. Not that she didn't have her own army tank–size SUV to run over to Lowery in, but I guess somehow them black Wranglers didn't look half as cute on a pedestrian. Besides, there was plenty of other towns out in the hill country, and Misty hadn't come close to trying them all. Yet.

And that's what I didn't get. If she was fixing to give Kennisaw boys another shot, what was she doing starting with the likes of me? After the Pawtuska game, I told Blaine it was kind of funny she didn't come down on the field with Rachel. Seemed like a sign she wasn't all that interested. Blaine just said, "Hey now, son. Where's your confidence? She's the lucky one to get to go out with *you.*"

He gave me a little punch in the arm. "I'll tell you what, Hamp, just follow my lead, and I'll have you stringing Misty Koonce along on a leash."

Now, I didn't care nothing about stringing anyone along on a leash, but setting there in Citronella's backseat, side by side with a girl that looked like Misty, I could think of plenty of things I did care about doing.

The plan was to hit Wild West Days over at Leonard

Biggins Park, but we didn't go straight there. Instead, we drove out to the edge of town where Blaine's cousin Jerry worked the evening shift at Big Jim's Little Store.

"A couple six-packs oughta cover us for now," Blaine said as he opened the door. "You got a five on you, Hamp?"

Truth be told, I wasn't exactly put out about postponing the trip out to the festival. More than likely Sara would be there with her folks, and the thought of running into them with Misty Koonce prancing along at my side didn't set right, even though there wasn't nothing official between me and Sara or really anything close to it. Still, I wasn't pumped up about stopping off for beer neither.

"We're in training," I told Blaine. "We don't need to be drinking no beers if we want to stay undefeated this season."

He just waved me off. "Maybe you don't, but me and the girls do, don't we, girls?"

The girls backed him up, and I didn't see nothing to do but fork over my five-dollar bill. "I sure hope you don't get caught driving and drinking that stuff."

Blaine laughed at that. "What do you think they're gonna do, throw their two best football players in jail? Give me a break."

But jail wasn't what I was thinking about. I was thinking about Sara and her father. If my dad got smacked into by a drunk driver instead of just running off to Sapulpa, I'd probably feel like hauling off and punching the next drunk driver I come across. I didn't even want to think about what Sara's eyes would look like if she found out I was riding around with two six-packs of beer. I'd ruther have her see me with Misty Koonce.

For a while, we drove the usual route around town, through

the Jolly Cone and down Main, up through the Wal-Mart parking lot and then back again. Misty didn't so much as take a sidelong glance my way the whole ride. Instead, every time we pulled through Jolly Cone, she craned her head out the window, looking back and forth and ordering Blaine to slow down.

"What the hell are you looking for?" Blaine finally said.

"Nothing," Misty said. "It's just there was some boys in here last week from Okalah that I got to talking to. They were characters. Real funny. Y'all would like 'em."

That didn't set good with Blaine. Ever since them Okalah boys cut his knee out last year, he couldn't even stand to hear the name of the town.

"Okalah?" He made it sound like a swear word. "If I ever seen one of them weak-ass cheaters in my town, I'd hit him so hard you'd have to call a plumber to come get my class ring out of his eye."

"What are you talking about?" Misty said. "You never even met these boys."

"Don't listen to him," Rachel said. "He hates everybody that's not from here."

"Not everybody." Blaine reached over and turned down the radio. You knew he was ready to argue then. "I just hate cheaters from Okalah. They're not like us over there. I'll bet they don't even have Christmas. They probably hang goat heads up on their doors and dance around on hot coals and drink pig blood."

"Oh, Blaine," Rachel said, all disgusted.

"I'm serious. They're the lowest form of life there is. Back in the old days, Kennisaw would've gone more than five un-defeated seasons if it hadn't been for Okalah's cheating. Did you know they had seven uncalled penalties in that game?"

Rachel crossed her arms and looked out the side window. "Yeah, you told me that about a hundred million times."

"And they had to wait till T. Roy graduated to get their cheating win in too."

"That was a long time ago," Misty said, leaning up towards the front seat. "These guys I met are different. They seemed like they'd be real fun to party with."

"Like hell." Blaine tipped his beer can up and took a good-size swig. "You know what kinda party I'd throw them boys if they come back through here? The kind where I'd knock 'em down and then pick 'em up by the scruff of the neck and drop-kick 'em one by one over the courthouse and all the way back to Okalah. You could watch 'em land headfirst on the pavement and go rolling down Main Street, bouncing off the parking meters like pinballs. That's the kinda party I'd throw 'em."

"Oh no, you wouldn't," Misty said. "You wouldn't do any such thing, not with these guys."

"Really? Well, I'll tell you what, why don't you talk to Randy Caine about what'll happen. Randy'll tell you all about it. You remember old Randy, don't ya, Hamp?" Blaine shot me a look in the rearview mirror.

"Yeah," I said. "I remember him." I didn't like talking about Randy much, though, not like Blaine did. Him and Blaine had got into it pretty bad a few weeks back, right after that lousy game against Kiowa Bluff when Blaine totaled up minus six yards rushing for the whole four quarters.

All Randy done was set on Citronella's hood out in the stadium parking lot. When he got off, there was a little teaspoon-size dent left where he'd been, and that was all it took to get Blaine up in his face. Randy was a pretty good-size boy hisself, and at first, he tried to play it off tough, cussing Blaine and saying one more dent wasn't going to make a difference to a hunk of junk like that old Blazer, but by the time he figured out that wasn't the right way to handle it, he was on the ground with a mouthful of grass and a chunk of broken concrete aimed at his head. I never seen Blaine go crazy like that the whole time I knew him. He was out of control. When Randy finally showed back up at school, one side of his head was shaved and he had him thirty-two stitches zigzagging down the pale skin there in a kind of lightning-bolt pattern. It wasn't pretty. Blaine just said, "He messed with the wrong guy." But I felt bad. I felt like there was something I should've done.

"God, Blaine," Rachel said, leaning her back against the car door and staring a hard one into him. "That's about all I hear out of you anymore, how you're gonna kick somebody's butt. I don't know what's got into you, but I'm sick of listening to it."

"Well, don't listen to it, then." He turned the radio up, loud.

"Oh, don't get that way." She turned the radio back down and scooted over towards him. "I just want to do something more fun. Like how about we go park somewhere and finish off our beers before we head over to the festival. You don't mind parking for a little while, do you?" She added a flirty note onto that last part.

He looked over at her, kind of checking out how the top buttons on her blouse was undone. "Okay," he said. "But I still don't want to see no Okalah boys around our town. That's all I can say."

We parked over on the dark side of the parking lot at Malcolm Hickey Elementary School, and Misty picked up what was left of one of the six-packs and said why didn't her and me head down to where the swing sets was and let Blaine and Rachel have a little time to themselves. So that's what we done.

The evening air was brisk and the moon was out big, and the pale light made Misty's hair look almost silver. I couldn't help but glance over at her time after time as we walked down to the playground. That hair of hers and her long eyelashes, the smooth skin along her neck and the way her furry pink sweater curved in the front. For a short girl with skinny arms, she filled that sweater out just about right.

I have to admit I felt proud to be with her. Course, she didn't have even a drop of any sad-soulful look in her eyes like Sara. Her eyes was more shiny, like toy money. And when she giggled, it was real high and thin like one of them little plastic pianos you get when you're about three years old. Right then, I didn't care, though. I could see myself strolling down senior hall with Misty on my arm, the other guys staring after us with their mouths hanging open, looking about like a pack of thirsty bird dogs, saying, "Look at who old Hampton's with. Boy, what I wouldn't give to be in his shoes."

No one would be making fun of the way I was with girls then. Blaine would slap me on the back and tell me I made the right choice, and next spring, him and Rachel and me and Misty would show up at the prom together dressed like red-carpet movie stars. No question, Blaine and Rachel was bound to be king and queen, but maybe me and Misty would be runner-ups, and we'd dance a slow one with the red and blue lights spinning around us and the rest of the school watching. Boy howdy. Now that's what it meant to be a Kennisaw Knight.

I hadn't even touched one beer, but watching Misty there under the moon like that, I felt a little drunk anyways. I couldn't help wondering if maybe I *was* falling in love with her after all. It was a different feeling than I got with Sara, but I didn't know much about this whole romance deal. Maybe you could fall in love with more than one girl at a time, only in two different ways. That wasn't exactly something I could ask Blaine or any of my other buddies about, though. They talked plenty about sex, but they never talked about love.

Anyways, I didn't want to be one of them types that can't stick to one relationship, like my dad or the way my mom was now. My mom. I didn't know what she was looking for, but it sure didn't seem like love. She flitted around from one man to the next the way a sparrow leaves one crumb in the dust and hops off to another one just 'cause it's different.

I swore to myself I wasn't never going to be like neither one of them, even if they was my parents. But here I was anyways with two girls burning up my mind—and about every other part of me too. Maybe T. Roy Strong went out with a different girl every night, but even just two in one week made me dizzy.

Down at the swing set, Misty drew her up a swing, and I set in the next one over. "You ever been to Dallas?" she asked, swaying back and forth in her swing.

I told her I'd been there once when I was a kid and Blaine's folks took us down, and she said, "Well, you oughta go back sometime. They got a mall with a skating rink inside. That's how big it is. They got a store with the cutest sandals and all sorts of fashions you can't get in Oklahoma."

"I don't wear cute sandals much," I said. I thought that was a pretty funny one right there, but she didn't pay much attention to it. Instead, she kept going on and on about the other cute stuff they had in Dallas, skirts and purses and ankle bracelets and everything else. Then she got going on movie-star hair and tanning salons, which somehow jumped over to her sister the cowgirl barrel racer. That girl could cover more subjects in a shorter amount of time than an all-in-one edition of the Funk & Wagnall's encyclopedia.

The whole time, she swang back and forth real slow, and I kept looking over at how low-cut that pink sweater of hers was. I told myself to quit it before she caught me, but next thing I knew, I'd be checking it out again. You would've thought I was hypnotized or something the way I kept at it. There's that old saying about a girl looking so good it hurts—well, I'm here to tell you that ain't no exaggeration.

Once, back when I was a little kid, I found me a brand-new razor blade on the ground. Course, a kid's bound to want to pick up anything so shiny and pretty, but the next thing I knew, blood was everywhere and I had a slice the size of the Grand Canyon across my palm. That's what being there with Misty reminded me of.

Sara wasn't like that. There wasn't nothing about being with Sara Reynolds that hurt. Fact was, with her, everything tended to get more clear, and my insides got more solid instead of frittering away into mush. Two different girls. Two different ways of feeling. They don't teach classes on that.

"You know what?" Misty stopped swinging. "There's something I always wanted, and maybe you can get it for me."

"Uh, sure." I looked down at her little red boots. "What is it?"

"A trophy. I always wanted me a trophy."

"A trophy?" I had to check her eyes now just to see if she was fooling, but she was as serious as the FBI.

"Everybody's got trophies but me. My sister's got her barrel-racing trophies. You and Blaine got your football trophies. Rachel's got her horse trophies for Mr. Highboy. I want one for something."

"Well," I said, mulling it over. "What are you good at?" I was only trying to be helpful, but she gave me a pooky look and let out a big sigh like she hadn't never seen anybody so backwards.

"I mean I want a trophy right now. I want you to get me one."

"What do you mean?" I said. "Are they giving trophies out at Wild West Days for something?"

"I don't know if they are or not." She climbed up out of the swing and walked over and stood with her legs straddled around mine. "But I know who does got some." She wrapped her hands around the swing chains, just touching mine, and leaned in so that low-cut sweater pooched out right under my chin.

"Who?" I said, trying not to swallow so hard she could hear it.

"Right up there." She nodded in the direction of the school building. "They got a whole case full of trophies doing nothing but setting there losing their shine."

"I helped win some of them trophies," I said.

She leaned in closer, and the smell of her perfume wrapped clean around my skull like some kind of beautiful poison from one of them deadly exotic flowers they got in the Amazon rain forest. "Well, then," she said, real soft. "In a way, I guess they belong to you already. All you gotta do is get one back and give it to me."

I glanced over her shoulder at old Malcolm Hickey Elementary. "I don't know. You mean break in there?"

She poked out her bottom lip. "Don't you think I'm worth it?"

"It's not that," I said. But then, I didn't know what it *was* neither. I didn't know much of anything right at that second, except how low-cut her sweater was and how sweet her perfume smelled and how her hands seemed to burn my skin where they touched.

"Just one trophy," she said, so close up her warm breath blew down on my forehead. "I'll never forget it."

"Okay," I said. "Just one."

CHAPTER THIRTEEN

Walking across that playground, I gave a look up at Citronella, hoping maybe Blaine and Rachel would be over there waving for us to come on, but whatever they was doing, they was doing it out of sight. That's how I was, wandering around looking for someone to make up my mind for me. It's like Sara said back in history class that time—if you don't know who you really are, how are you going to know what you think is right?

Misty skipped on up to the dark side of the building first and started checking for open windows. One after the next they was locked down tight, and I said we might as well give up, but she wasn't about to quit that easy. Finally, we got down to about the last two windows. I gave one a push, and it shot up so quick I thought it'd bust right there and spray broken glass all over us, but it didn't. It just stood there, wide open and dark as the devil's own cave. There wasn't no excuses left now. At least, that I could think of.

"Hey, all right!" Misty clapped her hands like she was about to go into a cheerleading routine. "Go on and climb up in there!"

I wasn't one bit excited about it myself, but I figured she was my date and it was my gentlemanly duty to climb in first. Once I got inside, I asked her if she was coming too, but she said she better stay there and be lookout, just in case. I didn't like that *just in case* business, but it wouldn't have been too gallant to go crawling back out now, not without at least looking for a trophy.

"Hey, Hampton, look at me," Misty whispered. She'd set her chin on the windowsill there so all I could see was her round little face grinning in at me. "I'm nothing but a head," she said, giggling.

And she did—she looked like a cut-off head someone done stuck up in the window for Halloween.

"Nothing but a head," she said again, and added on a haunted-house moaning sound to go with it. "Woooooo-ooooooh!"

Then she pulled her chin off the sill and said, "And make sure you get me a first-place trophy too."

That Misty. You couldn't help wondering what folks would've thought of her if she hadn't been so good-looking.

Once my eyes got adjusted, the room wasn't so dark. There was one of them glowing red exit signs out in the hall, and the light leaked in through the window in the door, washing up on the maps and the blackboard and the little desks. It was spooky, especially how small them desks was, all lined up in perfect rows like they was waiting for a bunch of dolls to show up for class. Out in the hall, they had the water fountain hung so low on the wall, I'd have to take a knee just to get myself a drink.

I had to shake my head over all that, wondering how I could've ever been small enough for a place like this. But I sure had been. This was my old school, where I'd grown up from a lost kid whose father run off on him to a first-team football player who's friends with the most popular kids around.

Heading down the hall, I had the feeling I was walking with all the children who come here down through the years. Same thing as when you walk out in an empty football stadium and you can practically see the players who played there and hear the fans cheering around you. Like being in the middle of ghosts, but in a good way. I couldn't help wondering if maybe pieces of people's spirits did somehow linger on behind them as they passed through life.

Funny, now that I done got out of reach of Misty's perfume, I was already starting to think like me again.

Something in the dark creaked and I froze. Probably just the building settling, I told myself, and started back down the hall. The trophy case was at the far end, lit up by the red glow of the other exit-sign light they had down there. The case stood right outside the old gym, and you could almost hear the squeak of kids' basketball shoes on the wood floor and the thump of dodge balls bouncing off the walls. It's odd, ain't it, how full up empty places can be?

That trophy case was sure something. Beautiful. Trophies going back to the T. Roy days, every different size you'd ever want—loving cups, gold balls, angels holding up gold torches, little football and baseball and basketball players froze in place, all with that red exit-sign glow settling down on them. Boy howdy. It wasn't just a collection of trophies, it was a whole *town* of trophies.

Then I seen it, that little old gold loving cup, setting way off in the corner gathering dust. It wasn't no more than four inches high, and the lettering on front read OUTSTANDING TEAMWORK. I liked that. Team*work*. Not team *spirit*, not *Rah, rah, we're the best and everyone else is a loser*. Not feeling big by looking at other folks like they was small. That's the easiest thing in the world to get tempted into, siding up with the better-than-everyones. I bet even a weed would call hisself a daisy if he could get away with it.

Teamwork, though, that's different. Everybody together, sweating from doing push-ups and running laps, scrimmaging and hitting the sleds, drill after drill, one guy backing up the other guy, going full bore right up till the last whistle and then jogging, all wore out, up the hill to the locker room. And everybody taking turns drinking. Working and working and working, then getting that drink—and it tastes sweeter than blackberry wine.

Trying. *Hard*. Helping each other to do better and better, and then running out on game day together and seeing what come of it.

There wasn't any putting into words everything that meant to me. It was about more than football, even, something that could last on past senior season. Suddenly, I wished Sara was there. She'd understand. She had a way of listening that was like she knew what you meant behind the words you said.

That's the thing. If you don't got someone to listen and

really understand, then it's like that deal about the tree falling in the forest and whuther it makes a noise even when no one's around to hear it. That's how I felt, anyways. There was so much I thought about that I never could tell anybody, and maybe it wasn't real in the first place if no one was around to understand it.

But Sara wasn't waiting outside the window. Misty was and she wanted her a trophy, not the meaning behind one.

Girls. They're a sight, ain't they?

Here I had one of them made me forget who I was, and the other one made me feel like who I really ought to be. I didn't know which was worse.

Now I was back to being confused all over. The smell of Misty's perfume come back to me and clouded up my head, even though she wasn't nowheres close. I started thinking maybe she *would* understand. Not as quick as Sara, but maybe if I just took this one little Outstanding Teamwork trophy out to her and explained about them ghosts in the hall and the low water fountains and short desks, she'd get it. She'd look up at me with them shiny blue eyes, soaking in everything I was telling her, thinking it was the deepest thing she ever heard, her little heart banging in her chest from what she was starting to feel for me.

And there I was. Hypnotized again.

The picture of how it'd be floated right up in front of me. I'd set down in one of them swings, and she'd straddle my lap and we'd kiss a long, head-turning kiss like they do on TV. Then, without me even having to ask, she'd stretch her arms up, and I'd pull that fuzzy pink sweater off over her head and unfasten her bra, and she'd undo the pearly buttons down the front of my shirt.

She'd say even with all them boys she dated from other towns, she hadn't never gone all the way, and I'd say I hadn't neither. I was just waiting for the right girl, I'd say, and then we'd have a first time like no one else ever had. It wouldn't be anything like what the other guys talked about when we cruised the streets in Citronella. Them and their converted basements. Next time they brought that up, all I'd have to do is nod and say, "Boys, you ain't got no more idea what you're talking about than a Sunday-school teacher knows how to cuss a good blue streak."

The trophy case didn't have nothing but a silver clasp lock to hold the sliding doors shut, so it wasn't no big deal to just pull out my house key and pry that little old thing off there in about a second flat. There was a fair damsel outside waiting, and if she wanted her a trophy, then a gallant knight like me durn sure had to get her one.

Still, I hated to break up that town of trophies, even if I wasn't taking nothing but a dusty four-incher that none of the kids was likely to miss. There was just a kind of spell about it I didn't want to snap. So I rearranged a couple of the bigger ones and clamped that lock back on and stood back and checked it over. I swear, fifteen state troopers couldn't have told the difference if you gave them a search warrant and police dog.

When I got back to the open window, I couldn't see Misty nowhere. "Hey," I whispered. "Misty? You out there? Wait'll you see what I got you."

But I still didn't see her when I landed down on the ground outside. She wasn't at the swings neither. I was standing there looking every which way when a giggle come tinkling down from somewhere. "Misty?" I said.

There she was, setting up on the slide on the other side of the monkey bars. "Where's my trophy?" she said.

"Right here." I held it up high, real proud of choosing the one on teamwork like I done.

She slid back down to the ground and dusted the seat of her britches off. "It's kind of little," she said.

"Wait'll you read what it says on the front," I told her.

She took the handle between her finger and thumb, holding it out kind of like she thought it might drip something nasty off on her. "Outstanding teamwork," she said. "Well, I guess that's better than worst teamwork."

"See," I said, "it's like a town full of trophies in there, and there's these little water fountains and desks and—"

"Come on," she cut in. "Let's get going. I want to get out to the festival before it's too late."

"Too late for what?" I asked.

"Just too late." She turned and headed on up the slope towards the parking lot.

When we got back to Citronella, Blaine and Rachel was setting about as far apart as they could. Blaine wasn't wearing his letter jacket now, and both of them's hair was messed up. They looked a little sweaty too, for how cool it was out.

"It's about time you two got back," Blaine said as we climbed inside.

"What's the matter with y'all?" Misty said, sliding over and leaning against the door.

"Nothing," Rachel said. "Except I guess Blaine forgot Knights was supposed to be gentlemen."

"Hey," Blaine said. "That's only when we got our letter jackets on. It wasn't my fault you skinned mine off me."

Misty laughed at that one. "That sounds like my kind of

gentleman," she said. Then she launched off on the topic of what schools had the prettiest letter jackets, and that turned into something about pants. I didn't listen to all she talked about, but there sure wasn't nothing in there about my trophy or teamwork or how it was to look for the meaning behind things.

Later on, we was cruising down Main, heading for the festival, and I noticed the trophy laying on the floorboard with the paper cups and beer cans and other trash. I wished I'd never even taken it out of the case then. I wanted to snatch it up and head back over to Malcolm Hickey and put it right back in with the other trophies where it belonged. But no one else was about to understand that, so I kept quiet and left it where it lay.

CHAPTER FOURTEEN

Over at Leonard Biggins Park, Wild West Days was in full swing. They had the same old carnival out there they always had with its sorry little merry-go-round and rickety Ferris wheel. On the north side, where we come in, the usual red, white, and blue refreshment stands was selling their pop and cotton candy and corn dogs and them huge brown turkey legs wrapped up in greasy paper napkins. Someone said one booth had fried Oreo cookies.

What that stuff had to do with the Wild West, I never did know. It's kind of hard to picture the Doolin gang riding around robbing trains and eating cotton candy and corn dogs and taking turns at the Ferris wheel. There was a big crowd out, though, and I don't guess they gave a day-old donut what any of it had to do with how wild the West was.

Blaine and Rachel and Misty walked ahead, and I trailed

back a little, swiveling my head this way and the other, on the lookout for Sara. It was a weird deal. I wanted to run into her and I didn't want to run into her at the same time. On the one hand, I always liked seeing her, but on the other, I was still supposed to be with Misty. Even if she didn't seem to much care whuther I tagged along or dropped down a hole, I figured I was obligated to her for the time being, anyways. How I'd explain that to Sara, I didn't know, but I was too big to hide, and something about her turned me too honest to lie, so I was going to have to explain somehow.

On the far side of the park, a good-size crowd done gathered round for the musical entertainment they had up on a bandstand in front of the pavilion. Some was cocked back in lawn chairs, but most was sprawled out on blankets or straight on the grass. We parked ourselves on an empty patch of ground at the back, and I set on the end of the row so I could keep on the lookout for Sara. Still wasn't no sign of her, and I got to thinking maybe her and her family already come and went. That probably would've been the lucky thing, but it was a disappointment to think about anyways.

A local country band was onstage. They was kind of old and so was their songs, but I didn't mind. Misty didn't make no secret out of how bored she was, though. We hadn't watched them ten minutes when she stretched out her arms and yawned and said she had to go visit the little girls' room. The porta-potties was on the other side of a line of oaks, and I watched her head off that way just to make sure she was all right. The way she swang that little butt of hers back and forth, she was sure worth watching for other reasons too, but I wasn't about to let my hormones get out of control over her no more now.

While I was looking off after her, I seen something I didn't notice before—an empty wheelchair parked on the grass way on the other side of the crowd. Sure enough, Mr. and Mrs. Reynolds was stretched out on a blanket in front of it, along with Sara's little sister, Lisa. Sara wasn't with them, but there was enough of an open spot left on that blanket that you could bet she'd been there sometime.

Now this don't make a bit of sense, but just the idea that Sara seen me come strolling along with Misty hit me about like a rusty hammer right in the chest bone. Wasn't no good reason for me to feel guilty like that. Me and Sara never even went out on a real date. We sure wasn't boyfriend and girlfriend. But somehow that didn't matter. I had to go find her and explain. That's how it was with Sara. I was always wanting to explain something to her, even when I didn't know exactly what it was.

She wasn't nowhere near the edges of the crowd or the line of oak trees or over by the Ferris wheel or merry-go-round, but just as I turned around the corner of the turkey-leg booth, I about run smack into her and her giant cup full of pop.

I stepped back and asked her if I made her spill any, and she looked down and said maybe just a little.

"Here," I said, reaching back for my wallet. "Let me get you another one."

"That's all right." She took a suck on her straw. "There's still plenty left."

So there we was, standing about a foot apart, and, course, everything I thought I'd explain to her flew right out of my mind, leaving my head about as empty as a birdhouse on a cold December day.

"Sure is a nice night out," she said.

And I didn't come back with nothing but, "Sure is."

I looked off down the row of refreshment stands, hoping maybe I'd see something down there worth talking about.

"Did you get out in time to see the bluegrass band?" she asked.

"Naw. I just been out here a little while." I was pretty sure saying *I* instead of *we* didn't exactly count as an official lie.

"They were a lot better than these guys playing now." She waved in the direction of where the band was. A different group was up now, younger with newer songs. "I can't stand this Top 40 stuff on the radio these days. My dad says it's like the polyester of country music."

I laughed. "I never thought of it like that. That's a good one."

She took another drag off her straw. "So," she said. "I guess you're out here with Misty Koonce?"

Just like that. She sure didn't beat around the bush none.

"Uh, yeah," I said. "But we're not *going out*, like dating or anything like that. I mean, it is a date, but it's just a fix-up kind of deal." I felt about like I was heading down a curvy road to nowhere, the way I was rambling around. "Does that even make any sense at all?"

"Sure," she said. "You're out, but you're not *going out*. You're on a date, but you're not *dating* dating." She cracked into a big grin, and we both got to laughing at how it sounded.

"Anyways," I said, "it was Blaine's idea. He got Rachel to set it up."

"You sure do hang around with Blaine a lot, don't you?"

"Yep," I said, kind of rocking back on my heels a little. I was always proud of being Blaine's best friend. "Me and old Blaine, we're about like brothers."

"Really?" She looked me square in the eye like she was sizing something up. "What makes you think that?"

That got me rocking back forward again. "What do you mean? That's what everyone says."

"But outside of playing football, y'all don't seem that much alike. I mean, for one thing, I wouldn't even think of trying to talk to Blaine about the things I could talk to you about. I don't even think he'd hear a word I was saying. You know?"

"Yeah, I know. He don't always listen real good. But you just gotta get to know him. We talk about a buncha stuff." I wanted Sara to like Blaine, same as I wanted him to like her. But standing there looking into them brown eyes, I could see she knew how it was. She knew I had a whole tangled woods worth of thoughts in me that my best buddy didn't have the first idea about.

She looked down and fiddled with the straw in her cup for a second, then looked me back in the eye. "I bet you don't talk to him about how you like to take walks in the country and watch the sun come up."

"No," I said. "I guess you're about the only one I talked to about that."

She gave that just a little bitty breath of a smile and said, "Well, you know what, the first time I saw you in eighth grade, when you came walking into math class, I could tell there was more to you than meets the eye."

"Yeah?" I rubbed my hand across the top of my head the way I do. "I guess I never was much to look at."

"I don't know about that." She looked away down the row of refreshment stands like maybe she didn't want me to see how big her smile had got now.

Right there, I felt like stepping over and hugging her. Wrapping her right up in my arms and telling her everything

I ever wanted to say to anyone. Probably scare her so bad she'd run home and lock the door for a week. Take out one of them stalker-restraining orders on me. Or maybe not. Maybe she'd have hugged me back and said, "Go on and tell it. Tell it all."

Course, I wasn't about to find out, not right then. Officially, I was still out on a date with Misty, and besides, I just didn't do things like that. But I figured I wouldn't be breaking no date rules if I at least said something about how I was thinking of taking me a good long walk out in the woods with a picnic lunch and wouldn't mind some company when I did.

"So," I started off. "I was thinking, you ever go out around Lake Hawkshaw much?"

"Oh, sure. We go out there and have picnics all the time."

"Well." I kind of shifted back and forth from one foot to the other. "They got a trail out there that leads through the woods and all the way up to these real great cliffs looking out over the lake. You ever hike up there any?"

"No," she said. "We don't do much hiking. My dad and all."

"That's right. I guess that was dumb."

"That's okay." She reached over and touched my arm real light just to show she didn't take no offense. "I'd like to hike up there. I bet it's beautiful in the fall."

"It sure is. You'd really like it." The only thing I had left to say was how about we both go out there together, but all the sudden, a hand clamped down on my arm and yanked me around the other direction.

It was Blaine, and he looked mad. "What are you doing over here?"

I started to explain, but he didn't let me get a half of it out.

"You know what's been happening while you was piddling around?" He didn't wait for me to answer that one neither. "C'mere and take a look."

He dragged me over about five yards so we could see past the corn-dog booth. At first, I didn't see what he was talking about, but then he pointed out this big oak way across the way, and there they was, three big boys and one little one all ganged around Misty Koonce.

"So what?" I said. For a second there, I guess I done forgot Misty was supposed to be my date.

It's guaranteed old Blaine didn't forget, though. His eyes flamed up hotter than a couple of Bunsen burners. "I'll tell you so *what*," he said. "Take a look at them red letter jackets over there. Okalah boys. Trying to snake your date right out from under you."

"Looks to me like they're just talking," I said. Truth be told, I wouldn't have minded if Misty did hook up with someone else. That way I wouldn't feel bad over how much I was enjoying talking to Sara when I was supposed to be on a date with another girl. Let Misty traipse off with them boys to Tucumcari, New Mexico, or anywheres else they wanted. I'd just stay here and hang with Sara till they folded the refreshment booths up and tore the Ferris wheel down. That'd be fine by me.

Course, Blaine didn't see it that way. He got going on how them Okalah characters was not only disrespecting me but the whole Knights team and the town of Kennisaw to boot. "You might let people walk all over you like that," he said. "But I ain't gonna let 'em get away with it."

You should've heard him. He was so full up with righteousness he might as well have been behind a high pulpit with one of them shiny blue robes on. Me, I didn't care so much if they did snake Misty off, but I had to admit them boys was showing some pretty hefty disrespect for us Kennisaw folk. Blaine had that pegged one hundred percent. Here I was, out on a date with Misty Koonce in her pink sweater, and these boys roll into our town, bent on hauling her off with them. For all they knew, I could've been in love with her too. Flat-out, jelly-legged, perfume-hypnotized, trophy-stealing in love. And they didn't care no more than if I was nothing but a little old ant trying to haul a bread crumb up a slick hill.

Man alive. The boys at school wouldn't never let me live that one down.

"Okalah's been pressing their luck against us for a long time." The way Blaine sounded, you'd have thought the whole town done him wrong someways instead of just a couple players. "I was gonna just wait and lay down the law on the football field, but when they come into our town, going after our girls, I ain't about to stand around and let 'em get away with that crap."

I didn't blame him for being mad about the way them boys cut his knee out on him, not one bit. It made me mad too. Course, the ones that really done it had already graduated and was gone by this season, but somehow that didn't make no difference right then. We was just thinking, *Buddy, if you're wearing a red letter jacket with an O pasted on front, you better look out.*

"So," Blaine said. "You coming, or am I gonna have to take care of this alone?"

I glanced back at Sara. The wind whipped her hair across her face, and she pulled it back. "What's going on?" she said.

"Don't worry," I told her. "This won't take long."

Just like that, I left her and took off after Blaine. How can you explain something like that? One second, I'm standing there talking to a brown-eyed girl about how pretty it is out around Lake Hawkshaw, and the next thing you know, I'm storming off across the park with my fists balled up.

"Let me do the talking," Blaine said when we was about halfway there.

"But she's my date."

He waved that off. "Don't matter. Just leave it to me and jump in when I need you."

"But we're just gonna talk to 'em, right?" I was already starting to lose some steam over the deal.

"Depends," Blaine said over his shoulder. He was walking out in front of me a little ways. It always bugged me when he done that. Made me feel like I wasn't nothing but a henchman. Like in the movies, how the gangster boss snaps his fingers at the big dumb guy and orders him to do the dirty work.

Over by Misty, the Okalah boys laughed at something. Judging from their size, I guessed they was a linebacker, two running backs, and a little free safety. The linebacker—a big meaty type with a blond crew cut and a wide red face—had his hand on her shoulder while the others stood around gawking at her chest like she was on TV or something instead of right there where she could catch them. Blaine was right—we didn't need these boys in our town. But that didn't mean we had to get in a fight or nothing. Best thing to do was just to shame them into slinking off with their tails between their legs. Blaine was an expert at that kind of thing, so I expected he had him a surefire speech ready to go. I should've known better.

Without saying word one, he barreled straight into their

little half circle, and just as the big blond linebacker turned his head, a fat old Romeo grin on his face, Blaine whipped a right so hard into his mouth the kid's knees buckled and he went down about like a Christmas tree the day after New Year.

Aw crap, I thought. *Here we go. Two of us against four of them.*

"What the hell?" the little free safety said. The running back next to him started towards Blaine, but I grabbed him by the jacket and slung him to the ground.

"Hey," Misty yelled. "What do you two think you're doing?"

Blaine just glared at the two kids left standing next to her and said, "We don't allow Okalah boys in our town, and we sure as hell don't let 'em talk to our girls." He stood there in his wide-legged stance with his fists clenched at his sides. "And we don't put up with sorry-ass football players that go for a guy's knees on purpose neither."

"I'll talk to anyone I want to," Misty said.

The running back I'd slung down was up on his feet again now, and the blond linebacker was up on one knee, dabbing at his lip with his fingertips.

"I'll talk to the man in the moon if I want to," Misty kept on. "You can't come in here and . . ."

Before she could finish, the linebacker launched up into Blaine's waist. Then the running back I'd grabbed before charged again, and I slung him right back down. The free safety stepped off to the side, but the second running back lunged in and clipped me a pretty good one on the ear. I shoved him backwards and hit him in the chest with a left and then a roundhouse right into his jaw. I was in the middle of it now. No last chances to choose any other ways. Arms and legs was flying everywhere, and a crowd come circling up, hooting and hollering, and little old Misty went to wailing like a siren going off.

Blaine was straddling the blond kid on the ground and the little free safety was kicking at him, but I had both the running backs on me, so my hands was too full to help him. We might've bit off more than we could chew, but Jake Sweet jumped in out of the crowd and took one of them boys off me. That would've been the end for the Okalah bunch right there, even if it was four of them against three of us, but Assistant Coach Liddell and Officer Longacre off the Kennisaw police force busted in and started pulling us off one another.

Officer Longacre made a barricade with his arms to hold three of the Okalah boys back, and Coach had a vise grip on my arm, but Blaine was still on the ground going after that blond kid. It was the Randy Caine deal all over again. Blaine's fist slammed up and down like an out-of-control crazy pumpjack, only it wasn't oil he was going for. I think it was something blacker than that even.

Finally, I guess Officer Longacre figured the rest of us wasn't as likely to kill anyone as Blaine was, so he grabbed the neck of Blaine's letter jacket and dragged him off, making sure to keep clear of swinging fists. There wasn't no fight left in the kid on the ground, though. He'd took it pretty bad. His face was a mess, blood streaming out of his nose and off his lips, and the flesh around his eyes already starting to swell up. He struggled to his feet, but he was still real shaky and kind of tilted over into his friends to keep from falling back down.

"You guys are such idiots," Misty yelled. She was so mad she was bawling.

I felt about like Jack the Ripper or somebody for doing that to her, but Blaine just looked at her and said, "Shut up, you little nitwit. You got it started. Tell her, Hamp."

I didn't say nothing, though. I was searching the crowd for Sara now. It hit me she probably followed us over and seen the whole business, and I couldn't have felt much lower over that idea if I was laying at the bottom of King Kong's grave.

Finally, I caught sight of her standing towards the back of the crowd. The wind was tugging at her hair, and her eyes wasn't just sad and soulful now. They was scared too. She turned around and walked off, and I didn't even try to follow her. Coach Liddell still had ahold of my arm, and besides, what was I going to say to her anyways? A girl like that don't go walking in the country with a Wild West Days brawler like me.

CHAPTER FIFTEEN

Sunday morning, a chilly gray mist hung low in the woods where we hunted, Blaine and his dad and me. Somewheres up ahead, they moved on, scaring up quail and talking football, while I lagged back by myself. I used to stick to Blaine and his dad about as tight as the skin on a peach, but lately I was wandering off by myself more and more. There was a deep gully over on the west side of the hunting lease that I liked to go to, and I found me my usual good smooth rock and set down to mull things over.

The gully was full of gold and brown leaves, but there wasn't no wind this early in the morning, so they just laid there still and damp instead of blowing up in curlicues like they done in the afternoon when the wind was up. There was birches and oaks and dogwoods and all sorts of trees out there. Little thorny vines and sticker bushes and blood-red sumac grew along the gully walls. There always was something about this place that cleaned my head out and made me think more clearer, if I could just get alone for a while.

I had a biology teacher this year, Miss Rose, and she was always going on about wildlife conservation. She was practically a nut on it. Sometimes I got to thinking maybe I might ruther do something in that line of work instead of football. I still didn't know what all it took to do it, but if you got to work outside in places like this, then that would suit me just fine.

After what happened out at Wild West Days, I figured the woods was the best place for me. Setting here on my rock with the good smell of the mist in the air and the trees looking down at me like wise old men, I could see how stupid I was. There wasn't no reason in the world for that fight. Sure, them boys needed to know they oughtn't to be talking to another guy's date, and Blaine had every right to make sure they understood we wasn't going to put up with no more knee-spearing from the Okalah Outlaws, but we could've spelled that out plainer than a first-grade reader without swinging fist one.

Truth be told, I was about fed up with myself. I didn't know why I couldn't be more the way I was on the football field out in real life. Like I say, on the field I was about as confident as they come. I'd do my time-freezing deal and see everything that needed doing in a split second. Then I'd walk out of the stadium, and the next thing you know I got Misty Koonce bawling to beat the west wind and Sara Reynolds looking at me like I'm Frankenstein.

Funny thing, though—standing there talking to Sara last

night, I really started to feel like I knew what was what. As good as if I was sizing up a third-down-and-five situation with a minute left on the clock. I was right on my way to asking her out, and I knew she'd go. What I wanted to know now was, why couldn't I make that feeling last?

The answer to that one didn't come to me, but I was bound and determined to figure it out one of these days. If I could just do that, then maybe I could freeze time outside them white chalk lines and know what to do right off instead of having to come here to the country and figure it out way after the smoke done already cleared.

Out in the woods, footsteps crunched along in the underbrush. It was Blaine. I could tell his footsteps anywheres. First thing I thought of was to reach for my shotgun so it didn't look like I wasn't doing nothing but staring off into space, but Blaine busted out into my clearing before I could get to it.

"I thought I'd find you over here again," he said. "What're you doing—waiting for the quail to come to you?"

"I was just taking a little time-out," I said. "Y'all must not have got much of anything. I didn't hear many shots."

Blaine leaned his Mossberg twelve-gauge against the same tree as my gun and took a squat next to me. "Naw," he said. "We didn't get as much hunting in as we did lecturing."

"About the fight last night?"

"Yeah." Blaine had him a couple of bacon, egg, and cheese biscuits wrapped up in his jacket pockets, and he pulled them out and handed me one. "I guess he figured the lecture he laid on me last night and the ones I got off Liddell and old Longacre wasn't enough. He was really on his high horse this morning."

"Well," I said, "a lecture's not so bad. At least he's not the yelling drill-sergeant type like Sweetpea and Jackie's old man." Sweetpea and Jackie was the Lewis brothers. Sometimes after practice or a game, you'd see old Mr. Lewis line them up against the side of his pickup truck like a couple of buck privates and just go to bawling them out so loud you could've heard him all the way down to Corpus Christi. Spit flying and his face about as purple as a bottle of grape Nehi.

"I don't know." Blaine took a bite of his biscuit. "With the yelling, you get it over and done with all at once. My old man's lectures, they just about go on forever. It's like the difference between hanging and the gas chamber. With hanging, the trapdoor drops open and—*boom*—you're gone. But with the gas chamber, you gotta set around and think about things while the poison clouds up around you real slow, and you start wishing you was already dead."

"Aw shoot," I said. "Your dad ain't that bad."

"Hell if he ain't. I bet if he had to he could talk for a month straight without setting down or taking a drink of water. And it's always the same old thing. He's the authority on everything and I don't know squat. They're all full of bull, if you ask me. My dad, Coach Liddell, Longacre, every one of 'em would've done the same thing in our place."

"You think so?" Setting there on my rock, I got this weird feeling like I was in two worlds at the same time. In one of them, I was here with Blaine, soaking up how mad he was over everything, and in the other one, I was still in the middle of them wise old men trees and that peaceful feeling they gave off.

"Sure they would." Blaine stared off past the gully. "I bet my old man would've chased 'em out of town with a shotgun back in his day. Now I gotta listen to him going on and on all about how we was lucky we was in Kennisaw. He said if we was in any other town when it happened, the law'd lock us up tighter than a can of Spam."

"Well, he was probably right about that, don't you think?"

"Maybe," Blaine said around his mouthful of egg and bacon and biscuit. "But we wasn't in another town." He swallowed. "That was the whole point. Them dudes come into our town. I'll tell you what, though, from now on, I ain't waiting for 'em to come in here first. If I have to, I'll drive right down the center of Okalah and kick every butt in sight, and I won't care the first thing what the law has to say about it."

"Hey," I said. "We'll get to kick their butts plenty on the football field."

"Yeah, well." Blaine swallowed again, hard this time. Them biscuits wasn't easy eating without milk to wash them down with. "To hear my old man talk, I might not even get to play in that game. He says if I get in any more trouble, I'll be lucky if the bleeding-heart English teachers up at school don't make Coach set me out for the rest of the season."

"What English teachers is he talking about? I see Mrs. Williams up at every game right on the fifty-yard line."

He didn't act like he even heard that. "Dad said if you wasn't involved in it too, they'd for sure set me out against Sawyer this Friday. Seems like the way he sees it, if they put me on the bench, they'd have to do it to you too, and Sawyer's too tough to beat without you in the lineup."

"Your dad said that?" It made me so proud Mr. Keller thought that way about me, I didn't see right off how it must've looked to Blaine.

"Yeah." He threw the tail end of his biscuit off in the high grass. "Like you was the only one the team needed, and I wasn't no more use than a flea collar on a dead dog."

"I'm sure he didn't mean it like that."

"I don't care how he meant it." He stood up and shoved his hands in his pockets. "They ain't taking me out against Sawyer or Okalah either one. We gotta win them games. There ain't no other option. And I'm gonna be the one to win 'em for us too."

He stepped over and picked up his twelve-gauge. "C'mon. Let's go. There ain't nothing around here worth shooting." He started off through the high brush and I got my gun and followed along after him like I'd been doing since we was nine years old and heading through Leonard Biggins Park to see T. Roy Strong.

CHAPTER SIXTEEN

Friday night, when we busted through that paper banner and charged onto the field, the crowd let loose with cheers so loud they about rocked that old stadium clean off the ground. Our last two games of the regular season was homers, this one against Sawyer and the next one against Okalah. Course, we had us a longtime grudge against Okalah, but everybody knew Sawyer was really our toughest opponent in the division, so there couldn't have been any more electricity running through the stands if they'd been hooked up to the Hoover Dam. It was almost enough to burn out all the bad feelings I'd felt since that stupid fight.

First time I seen Misty at school after that night, she just hugged her books against her chest and turned her nose off in the other direction. I figured that was lucky. If she'd said what she was thinking, it would've probably scorched me down into a pile of smoking cinders right there in the middle of senior hall. Sara did at least look at me when I come into history, but truth be told, I didn't have the nerve to meet her eye to eye, and even when we got in our study group, I kept shut up. You would've thought I'd come up with some explanation for her in a week's time, but no way. Not me.

I didn't have time to think about any of that stuff now, though, not with a team like the Sawyer Comets staring us down from the far side of the field.

In the last three years, Sawyer done beat every team they played but one, the Kennisaw Knights. And in all that time, we never won by any more than six points. Now, we'd lost over half our starters from last season to graduation, but Sawyer still had every single one of their offensive stars, and that included Anton Mack, their tailback. He was pretty good last year, but this year he was crazy good. Word was, he didn't just have every move in the book, he had enough for a whole encyclopedia.

What no one on our team ever talked about, though, even Jake Sweet, was how Mack looked like he was aiming to break Blaine's single-season rushing record. He could even do it tonight, but he'd have to go through me, and I was bound and determined not to let that happen. Maybe I didn't know how to fix things up with Sara Reynolds, but there wasn't no one in our division knew how to tackle better than me.

Leastways, there hadn't been before this season.

Thing was, Anton Mack wasn't the only Sawyer star folks was talking about. On defense they had this big Kiowa Indian boy named James Thunderhorse who moved down from Shawnee. I mean, this kid was a mountain, only a junior and already six five and almost three hundred pounds. The Kennisaw sports page called this game "the closest thing to a Super Bowl that 4A football was likely to see," and on top of that they put in a whole article about who was better on defense, James Thunderhorse or me. Said it was a shame me and him wouldn't be on the field at the same time battling it out, 'cause that'd be the best heavyweight matchup since Joe Frazier and Muhammad Ali.

The *Kennisaw Sun* wasn't the only one interested neither. Rumor was that writers from the big papers up in Oklahoma City and Tulsa, maybe even Dallas, would be in the stands this Friday night. Blaine said that meant there'd probably be scouts from OU and OSU coming around too. He said he hoped they did, 'cause he planned on putting on a show they'd still be talking about on signing day.

Now, I know his head told him that was true. His head told him he was still the best damn runner on the best damn team in the hill country. But the gut don't always believe what the head wants it to.

We won the coin toss and took the opening kick. Seven downs later Sawyer stopped us cold and we had to punt. Then our defense come on the field and we stopped them dead, and that's the way it went for most of the first half. A defensive battle. Anton Mack might've had every move in the book, but I'll tell you what, once I got a good look, I felt like I'd done read that book cover to cover and back again. Just watch his hips. Don't get fooled by all that flashy foot-work. Watch them hips and they'll tell you where he's fixing to go every time. Play after play I was right there to stop him, and when I did, them stands would bust into their chant of "Hampton! Hampton! Hampton!"

Only thing was, them newspaper stories wasn't wrong about James Thunderhorse. When our offense took the field, he ate us up. If we tried to pass, half the time he'd bust through and smush Darnell about as flat as the jack of diamonds, and the rest of the time he'd put so much pressure on, Darnell had to throw the ball away. And there just wasn't no running to his side at all. Blaine was getting off faster than I seen him all season, but he didn't have nowhere to go. Once he grabbed me as I was jogging onto the field and said, "Damn, it's like I'm a Ferrari running head-on into a concrete wall at eighty miles an hour."

And then it got worse.

With about twenty seconds left in the first half, old James Thunderhorse turned into more than a hunk of concrete. Now he was the Ferrari. If Ferrari made semi trucks. It was a pass play from the shotgun. We had our guard and tackle both teamed up on Thunderhorse, but even the two of them wasn't no match for him, and he come barreling through with no one to stop him but Blaine.

Right here, I want to say that something Blaine never got enough credit for was his blocking. That boy always could block with the best of them. And I should know 'cause he took me out more than a few times in practice. Sure, he set him a bunch of running records last season, so you might figure he wouldn't fool with the nuts-and-bolts stuff that don't have no glory in it, but when it come to football, Blaine was one hundred percent serious about everything he done.

So it was just Blaine between Thunderhorse and Darnell. Fifteen yards downfield, Jake Sweet was trying to shake loose and get in the open. Blaine put his head down and drove straight into Thunderhorse's gut. His technique was perfect.

He done everything a blocker could do, except hit his man over the head with a monkey wrench. But it wasn't enough. The next thing he knew he was flat on his back with that big old tackle's cleats pushing off his chest.

After that, Thunderhorse slammed into Darnell so hard you would've thought from the sound of it someone fired off a twelve-gauge shotgun. And then, there it was, the ball spinning through the air. Fumble. Once the durn thing hit the ground and took off bouncing, it was way out of Blaine's reach. Darnell was about half knocked out, so Thunderhorse didn't have no competition and dove on top of it just before Sweetpea and three of our other guys jumped on top of him.

Sawyer's ball on the twenty-yard line.

Boy howdy. From the moan that come out of the crowd right then you would've thought they just found out the end of the world was coming a week from Sunday.

Time was running out in the first half, and I did what I could to block the field-goal attempt, but their kicker got the ball up high and fast, and it popped through the uprights sure as a poke in the eye. Sawyer had three points to our zip.

Thunderhorse done it. He set up the go-ahead score.

As we was running off the field at halftime, Blaine bumped his shoulder pad into me and said, "Looks like you're gonna be sharing headlines from now on."

I just looked at him and said, "The only headline I care about is the one that says 'Kennisaw Wins.'"

"That's all right," he said. "I'll take care of that one."

CHAPTER SEVENTEEN

The second half, defense ruled again. Once Anton Mack did get loose around left end for a twenty-five-yarder, but other than that one, we made good and sure he wasn't anywheres near beating Blaine's record, at least not tonight. Course, on the other hand, old James Thunderhorse made good and sure our offense didn't get down the road any farther than a pickup truck with three flat tires, so we was about even.

Except for that three-pointer Sawyer picked up in the first half.

I know Blaine had to be thinking about that too. If something didn't change real quick, folks was bound to forget just about everything but how James Thunderhorse knocked him back on his butt on the way to setting up that field goal. The one puny little field goal that busted our fifth undefeated season slick as lightning through a dead oak.

By the fourth quarter things was starting to look pretty dark. Then, with only about six minutes left in the game, Coach Huff pulled a flea-flicker out of his bag of tricks. We hadn't run this play no more than two or three times in practice, but we sure needed something, and this was about our last chance. Darnell took the snap in the shotgun, faked like he was fixing to roll out on Thunderhorse's side, but then stopped and pitched the ball to Blaine. Blaine charged up like he was taking it around left end, and then when Sawyer's secondary darted in to plug up the run, he screeched to a stop and launched off a long bomb. He threw it a little too far, but old Jake stretched out and pulled it in with one hand, crashing down right on Sawyer's forty-yard line.

The crowd went crazy and so did I. And you should've seen Jake. He popped up from the ground and scampered around in a circle, holding the ball up like he just found out it was made out of gold or something. He wasn't always the best receiver in the world, but no one was ever going to call him Skillethands again after that play.

The whole offense was charged up now. This was huge. Nobody could stop Kennisaw if we got inside the forty. That's what we all thought, anyways, but we hadn't come up against James Thunderhorse before. Three plays later, Coach Huff was calling for another punt.

There wasn't nothing wrong with that strategy. Kick it down inside the ten and let the defense take over. We'd done held Sawyer all night, and there was plenty of time left for our offense to get the ball back and score. Blaine didn't like it, though. He ripped off his helmet and charged right up to Coach and started yelling, "What are you doing? We can't punt. Give me the ball. You gotta give me the ball. I can make it!"

Coach wouldn't have none of it, though. He told Blaine to get back in there in punt formation or he'd yank him clean out of the game.

"That's chicken shit," Blaine said. He kind of muttered it as he turned around, but I heard him plain as day.

Coach grabbed his jersey and got right in his face then. "What'd you say, Keller?"

From the look on Blaine's face, I thought sure he was fixing to come out with it again. That would've been it too. You can bet Coach would've benched him right on the spot. Blaine knew it too. He didn't really swallow his pride, though. That'd be too much to expect out of a proud guy like Blaine, but he didn't say "chicken shit" again neither. He just stared into Coach's eyes and said, "All I want's a chance, Coach. That's all. Just a chance."

Coach let go of his jersey. "You'll get it," he said, "when the defense takes the ball back for us. Now get out there in punt formation."

Blaine went ahead and run back out there, and it's a good thing too. That punt turned out better than even Coach could've predicted when Tommy Nguyen downed it on the two-yard line. You got to know Blaine was still thinking it wasn't the true Kennisaw way to play, but even he couldn't argue with the fact that Sawyer had their backs up against it. They was going to have to run plays right out of their own end zone, and even the littlest piddling mistake could turn the tide now.

It was Sawyer's turn to come up with a surprise play, and that's just what they done. And I'll tell you what, if the crowd wasn't already up on their feet, they would've sure got there when old James Thunderhorse run out onto the field to play offensive tackle.

Truth be told, it really didn't surprise me that much. It was the smart thing to do. A lot of guys played both ways in 4A football. And they hadn't been able to keep me out of their backfield all night, so there wasn't no other choice but to stick the big man out there and bull it out of the shadow of the goalpost. Thing was, though, that meant we knew exactly what to expect.

Sure enough, they run it off-tackle, but Thunderhorse wasn't as used to blocking as he was to tackling and got his posture too erect. You just can't do that. I seen it right off and knocked that big old boy clean back on his butt and hauled Anton Mack down on the half-yard line. That got the crowd going all over again with "Hampton! Hampton! Hampton!"

Thunderhorse was a quick learner, though. He wasn't about to make that mistake again. Second down, the center snapped the ball, the quarterback turned, faked a handoff to Mack, and then followed him into the line right behind their big giant tackle. Both Mack and Thunderhorse was gunning for me, and this time Thunderhorse stayed low. There wasn't going to be no knocking him on his butt now, so what I done was, I jumped up as high above that line as I could, knowing full well his shoulder pad was fixing to blast into my thigh like a runaway train.

There I was, up in the air, my feet spinning up to where my head ought to have been, and that's when I done it. I stopped time. The Sawyer quarterback froze in the little bitty pocket of space behind Mack, who was driving into Thunderhorse, helping him drive into me. Everything was clear as sunup in June. The QB tilting his head down, tucking his shoulder, planting his left foot, ready to push off for a cut back to the right, the ball cradled in his right arm. I could make out the laces in the leather, each one of them, and even spinning end over end like I was, it was the easiest thing in the world to hammer down and punch the ball loose. Then at the same time, I jackknifed my body right into that quarterback's chest so he couldn't get the recovery neither.

Time flashed back to full speed and I slammed into the ground, the quarterback and Mack both crashing down with me. And there the ball was, spinning like a top right in front of my face.

Now, if you never been in a dog pile, let me tell you, you don't want to get in one if you can any way avoid it. It's the cussingest, gougingest, spittingest, pullingest, pokingest, pinchingest, punchingest place there ever was. And from the feel of it, I had everybody on both teams squirming around on top of me too. I think I could've recited "Gunga Din" a hundred times forwards and backwards before them officials finally got all them boys sorted out and pulled off, but when I finally rose up with the football squeezed against my gut, the crowd whooped so loud it sounded about like an A-bomb going off.

Kennisaw's ball on the one-yard line. Blaine was fixing to get his chance just like Coach told him.

CHAPTER EIGHTEEN

Blaine always was one of them guys that liked pressure when it come to football. Whuther it was fourth and three or third and goal with a second left on the clock, he wanted his number called. Jevon Woolsey, our quarterback last season, used to call Blaine "Money," short for "Money in the Bank," 'cause it was a sure thing Blaine'd pick up a first down or a touchdown when you had to have it. This one time against Kiowa Bluff, we needed us five yards for a score, but Blaine didn't just run five yards. With all the cuts and dodges and whirls and twirls, going towards one sideline then back towards the other, he must've run a solid mile before he finally slammed it over the goal line. Old Money Keller. That was the perfect nickname.

But, like I say, that was last season.

Tonight we had us one yard to score and take the lead, and instead of calling Blaine's number right off, Coach called for a quarterback sneak. On first *and* second down. I expected Blaine to blow up, but he didn't say nothing. You can always tell when he's pissed off on the football field, though, the way he jams his hands on his hips and stamps around with them little short, sharp steps. And you couldn't blame him neither. Coach had pretty much promised he'd get his chance, and now two downs went by, and no matter how strong and shifty Darnell was, we hadn't pushed the ball a single inch closer to pay dirt.

I never was one to go to coaching the coach, but this time I had to say something. Coach Huff had just signaled in for a time-out, and I stepped up and told him straight-out that we needed to put the ball in Blaine's hands. Coach looked me up and down kind of squint-eyed like some bug had lit down beside him and he was wondering how come it could talk. "You think so, do you, Green?" he said, turning back towards the field. "Well, I'll take that into consideration."

That was that. But when our offense gathered up around him, the first thing out of his mouth was, "Keller, do you still think you can make it?"

Blaine matched his stare and then some. "Just give me the ball," he said.

Coach banged the side of his helmet. "You got it."

It was a running play off left tackle, *away* from James Thunderhorse. Problem was, all night Thunderhorse had done pulled over and dragged Blaine down no matter where he tried to go. There just wasn't enough speed left in that knee of his for Blaine to bust away. If he wanted to score this time, he'd have to grind in there on nothing but raw guts.

Our boys lined up in the I, and Darnell started his count. On the other side of the line of scrimmage, a Sawyer linebacker darted up behind left tackle, getting ready for a run to come that way. Too late for any audible now. Sweetpea snapped the ball, and Blaine charged off and took it from Darnell with perfect timing. Our line was doing everything they could up front, but that durn linebacker already sealed the gap, and Thunderhorse was pulling around. If Blaine kept charging, he'd run smack into that same concrete wall he'd run into all night. If he tried to cut back, them slow feet of his wouldn't never get him around the end in time. It looked like every possible route into the end zone was blocked off.

So he done the impossible. He flew.

At the very last second before hitting that sealed-up line, he launched off like a fighter jet and ripped over our tackle *and* the Sawyer linebacker, ricocheted off James Thunderhorse, and finally skidded shoulder-first into the grass on the far side of the goal line.

Touchdown.

Another A-bomb exploded in the stands.

Officially, the game still had almost three minutes left, but unofficially, it was over and ready for the history books. You could see in the way them Sawyer boys carried themselves they was deflated. Their offense hadn't done much against us all night and they sure didn't get no first downs once they got the ball back. The only thing we had to do then was run out the clock. The crowd counted it down at the very end: "Five, four, three, two, one." The bomb that went off then nearly brung that old stadium to the ground.

Our whole team tumbled over each other in a pile that was just about as rough as the one I was under when I recovered that fumble, but it was a kind of rough that felt a whole lot better. Once we got up and shook hands with them poor old Sawyer boys, Blaine ripped his helmet off and led us over to the sidelines to salute the fans, and more than that—to just stand there and soak up all the love pouring down. You should've seen the smile on his face. It was about as big as the bottom end of a tractor wheel. He done it. He scored the winning touchdown. His old man couldn't come up with no lectures to ruin that.

He slammed me a hard one on the shoulder pad. "How about it, Hamp," he yelled in my ear. "Do you see any of 'em?"

"Any of who?" I yelled back. For a second I thought he meant girls, like Sara Reynolds, maybe, but course that wasn't what he had in mind at all.

"College scouts!" he hollered. "College scouts and big-city sports writers."

I scanned the crowd, but what I seen was even stranger than spotting college scouts or sports writers or even Sara Reynolds. It was my mom.

There she was, right on the front row, smiling and waving to get my attention, calling my name out.

"Well, what do you know," Blaine said. "Your mom's up there."

"Yep," I said. "First time in two years."

"Who's she with?"

I checked next to her, expecting to see Jim Houck from Lowery, but instead of him there was a big tall guy with gray hair combed back and curling down long behind his ears.

"I don't know," I said, my voice mostly drowned out by the cheers. "I never seen that one before."

Right about that time, the rest of the boys on our team and

CHAPTER NINETEEN

That night after we showered and drove around town and relived that Sawyer game about as much as we could stand, I headed on back to the house, even though I'd have ruther done just about anything than walk in there and see my mom with her latest man. Funny thing, though, soon as I stepped up on the porch I got a different feeling than usual. Instead of one of them prehistoric old Fleetwood Mac songs leaking out the door, one of *my* favorite songs was playing, and then when I opened the door, the strangest thing yet happened. Before I even got a foot inside, my mom sung out with, "Welcome home, hero!" and went to hopping up and down like her shoes was on fire. I tell you what, it about knocked me right back off the porch into the bushes.

She was over there behind the coffee table next to that

same man I seen her at the game with, but they wasn't in the middle of slow dancing or nothing. And she wasn't waving around no whiskey glass or playing cards or Scrabble or any of the other hundred and fifteen ways she usually had of ignoring me when I come in from someplace. The coffee table was laid out with a big old platter of chicken wings and then there was some tortilla chips and bean dip and a whole big bottle of orange pop. All my favorites.

"What's going on?" I said, still standing in the doorway like maybe I shown up at the wrong place somehow.

"Well, don't look so surprised," she said. "Can't a mother throw a little celebration for her boy when he plays the best game of football this town's ever seen? Now shut the door and come on over here and give your mom a hug."

I went ahead and done like she said, but that hug felt a little on the stiff side, the way hugs do, I guess, when you don't get a lot of practice in on them. So far, I still hadn't quite figured out what was going on, but then Mom introduced the man next to her. His name was Tommy Don Coleridge. He'd played him a little football back in the day, and he was the one that thought I had such a good game out there tonight.

So that's it, I thought. *Mom met her a big football fan, so now she's fixing to be one too.*

Tommy Don gave me a big friendly smile and a firm handshake, but not one of them vise-grip handshakes like Jim Houck tried on me. There wasn't nothing for him to prove since he was a pretty big boy hisself, every bit as tall as me, and I'm six foot four. With that long gray hair swept back behind his ears and them happy crinkles around his eyes, he was a far cry from the old hotshot car salesman. I had him figured for a house painter, the way he was dressed—denim work shirt, faded blue jeans, and old work boots all spattered up with different colors of paint.

"I'll tell you what," Tommy Don said. "That game you played out there tonight was the best I've seen in high school football. And I've seen some pretty good games."

Mom put her hand up on his shoulder. "Tommy Don used to play right here in Kennisaw, and now he's moved back to town for a while, and it was the funniest thing." She let out one of her little girly giggles. "There I was working at the store and just happened to look up and here he came strolling in big as you please right up to the counter where I was working."

Same old story. That dollar store might just as well have been a professional dating service, the way my mom worked it. Right then, I even felt a little bad for Tommy Don Coleridge. Six months tops before she'd dump him like she done all the others.

Thing was, though, you couldn't feel sorry for Tommy Don for long. He was just too confident and comfortable with hisself for that. Instead of Mom shooing me off to the back room like usual, we all set down to the coffee-table snacks, and he went to telling stories and cracking jokes that made you feel like you known him for ten years instead of ten minutes. Football talk wasn't the half of it neither. Once we got that out of the way, it was fishing and rock climbing, scuba diving and flying. Then Italy and museums, books, paintings, and concerts. He'd seen Fleetwood Mac three times live. I thought Mom was fixing to faint dead away into the bean dip when she heard that one.

But Tommy Don didn't do all the talking. No sir. He had a way of keeping everyone included in the conversation, asking the kind of questions you wanted to answer instead of cringing over. No one was left out with Tommy Don around. By the time he finally said he'd better get moving along, that old room done felt like something it hadn't really been since the first day we moved in—a family room.

Later, when I was laying in bed, I just about couldn't stop grinning. This was one of the best days I could remember. First, I got out there and played the game of my life, and now maybe my mom had finally found her someone decent that she could get back to being her old self around. Someone she could stick with. And I figured if she could do it, I could find me a someone like that too. Matter of fact, if I hadn't done blown it, I might've found her already.

For a long time, football was about the only thing in my life that seemed like anything could come of it. Now the whole world was a great big garden fixing to bloom right up to my eyebrows. And that feeling lasted clean through all my dreams that night and through the morning before it finally come unraveled the next afternoon.

CHAPTER TWENTY

Saturday afternoons Blaine and me was allowed in the Rusty Nail Tavern out on Route Thirty-three so we could watch the college games in there with the grown men. There wasn't nothing fancy about the Nail and that's a fact. A couple of raggedy beer-stained pool tables, a dartboard, and posters of beer girls in bikinis up on the walls. Everything was pretty dingy except for the big-screen TV. They spent them some tall dollars on that bad boy.

You couldn't help but feel like you was riding high, setting in there with the men in their flannel shirts and fishing caps. Norman the bartender even let us split a pitcher of beer, but I didn't drink no more than a sip, so Blaine got the most of it. That day, after our win over Sawyer, the whole place was about as rowdy as a box full of wild dogs. Beer bottles rattling, smoke swirling around under the ceiling fans, the TV cranked up high, and men's voices cranked up higher than that. Several of them old boys was waving copies of the morning sports page around, quoting off their favorite lines and making up some of their own. Boy howdy. A stranger walking in would've thought someone just won a world championship, a Cadillac, and a date with Miss America all at the same time.

The only one that wasn't about fit to sail over the roof was Blaine. Problem was, none of them sports pages from the big city papers or even the *Kennisaw Sun* gave him the kind of credit he figured he deserved. We'd got together that morning to pick us up some copies of the Oklahoma City and Tulsa papers and set down at Sweet's Café to read them out loud to each other over a couple big stacks of blueberry pancakes. Now, I ain't going to get to bragging over the stories them papers done on me, but let me just say they was pretty durn good. Blaine, though, wasn't none too happy over how they shortchanged him.

"Can you believe these fools?" he said, slamming the sports page down on the tabletop so hard the saltshaker just about jumped over the syrup. "They hardly even mentioned me, and this one here got my name spelled wrong."

"What do you mean?" I said. "They wrote up the whole thing about you throwing that long bomb and diving over the goal line for the game winner. See, it's right here."

"Yeah, but there oughta be more than that. Guy wins the damn game, you oughta have a whole article on him the way they got them extra ones on you."

"Aw," I said. "It ain't that big a deal. They just wrote me up a little bit more 'cause they'd done built up on who was better, me or James Thunderhorse."

"Buncha yokels." Blaine looked down at the paper, shaking his head at it like it was the pitifulest thing he ever seen. "I just hope there was some college scouts out there. Anyone who really understands football's gonna know who saved our undefeated season for us."

So you can bet Blaine wasn't joining in when the Rusty Nail boys started flashing their newspapers around, and it didn't get no better when J. M. Pierce set down at our table and asked me whuther I heard from Coach Huff yet today.

I told him I was out all morning and hadn't heard from nobody, and he just looked at me and said, "Man alive, son, you mean to say you don't know OU and OSU both called him this morning wanting game film on you?"

Blaine perked up at that. "Who said?"

"*He* said. Coach Huff hisself. I talked to him not more'n an hour ago."

"Well," I said, "if they wanted game film, then I'm sure they didn't want it just on me."

J. M. gaped at me like I was crazy. "Who else would they want it for?"

"The whole team probably." I glanced over at Blaine, but he turned away.

"I tell you what, Hamp," Carl Avery put in over my shoulder. "Don't pay no attention to them OSU boys. You go on up to OU. That's where you need to be. At the top of the top."

"That's right," J. M. said. "After that game last night you can write your own ticket to any program you want to go to."

That got the others to flapping their lips, agreeing with Carl. And that was all right. It's good to have folks on your side like that, but then J. M. had to go and clap Blaine on the shoulder and say, "You know what, son? You better be good to Hampton. Maybe he'll put in a word for you with some of them OU scouts when the time comes."

Blaine flinched away from J. M.'s hand a little, like maybe it was infected with the chicken pox or something, but he didn't say anything back. He just locked his jaws and stared into the side of his beer mug.

"Hey now," I said. "Blaine ain't got nothing to worry about." It was weird. All the sudden my voice sounded like it belonged to somebody else. I wasn't used to talking up in a group of men that way. Blaine usually did most of the talking for both of us. "In case none of y'all noticed," I went on, "Blaine's the one scored the winning points last night."

"Yeah," Carl said. "After you put him down there on the one-yard line."

A couple of the others chimed in with how they hadn't never seen nothing like the way I handled James Thunderhorse down there at the goal line, and J. M. said, "Besides, it don't matter if we noticed who scored that touchdown. The real question is, did the *scouts* notice?"

That got a couple of laughs and a hoot out of Carl, so I set right up straight and said, "I'll tell y'all what, if it wasn't for Blaine, old James Thunderhorse would've probably tore me up worse than an alligator gar on a minnow. Blaine taught me everything about football I know. I wouldn't even be playing on this team if it wasn't for him."

"Maybe they oughta train him to be a coach, then," Carl said, " 'cause he sure ain't fast enough for a running back."

Some more laughs come on that one, and J. M. gave Blaine's shoulder a nudge. "Hey, maybe Oral Roberts University will call up, wanting game film on you."

"Now, Jim," Carl said. "You know Oral Roberts ain't got a football team."

"I know, but they might want him for the glee club. Haw!"

The whole room went to guffawing over that, but still Blaine set there without a word, just white-knuckle squeezing on that beer mug so hard you would've thought it was fixing to bust right in his hand.

"Now wait a minute." I tried to get as much force into my voice this time as I could. "Them colleges better keep in mind that me and Blaine's a team. Always have been since I moved here. And I ain't about to go off to no school that don't see that. 'Cause I tell you what, the two of us are unstoppable. Anywhere, anytime. Ain't that right, Blaine?"

"Sure," he said, still not looking up. "That's right."

"Damn right, that's right," I said.

"Just do me this one favor." Blaine finally raised his head and looked me straight in the eye. "Tell your mom not to drag that fool she was with last night out to any more of our games. He don't belong there."

That just about knocked me out of my chair. Maybe Blaine didn't warm up too good to the idea of me trying to take up for him, but that wasn't no call to turn around and snap out something about my mother.

"Who you talking about?" I said when I got my tongue to working again.

Blaine's eyes narrowed to little slits. "You know who I'm talking about."

"Your mom was out with someone at the game?" Carl asked. He sounded jealous. There was a time when he tried getting Mom to go out with him, but for all the men she dated, she never did include no married ones in there.

"You must be talking about Tommy Don Coleridge," Norman the bartender said. "I seen him out there with her. I didn't even know he was back in town."

"He's back, all right," J. M. said. "I heard he come back broke and had to move in with his old man."

"That figures," Norman said.

"Wasn't he a Buddhist for a while?" Carl asked, but no one jumped in to verify that one.

"He always was a crazy bastard," Norman said. "I'm surprised he's even still alive."

Everything was flying by me so fast, I couldn't hardly grab ahold of any of it, but I knew what they was saying didn't sound the first thing like the man I met yesterday.

"He seemed all right to me," I said, shooting a quick glance towards Blaine. He just set there, turning his beer mug in a little circle on the table, a look in his eyes like he had more on his mind than he was coming out with right now.

"Don't let Tommy Don Coleridge fool you," Haywood Ritter said from the next table over. With that white walrus mustache and them wild bushy eyebrows, Haywood was the oldest one in the room, and he was the most respected out of any of them too. Not 'cause of his age but 'cause he was the cousin of T. Roy Strong. "I wouldn't trust Tommy Don any farther than I can spit," he said.

"Maybe he's changed since you knew him," I said, but old Haywood shook his head.

"People don't change."

"That's right," Blaine added for good measure. "Once you're a loser, you're always a loser."

CHAPTER TWENTY-ONE

On the ride home from the Rusty Nail, I didn't have nothing to say to Blaine till we turned down Mission Road, and then I just had to come right out and ask it. "Why'd you say that about my mom back there?"

Blaine kept on staring ahead. "I didn't say it about your mom. I said it about that jerk she was with. You needed to know what kind of company she's keeping."

"You didn't have to say nothing in front of everybody like that." I looked out the side window at the row of run-down gray houses. "Besides, I ain't got no say over who she goes out with."

"Well, maybe it's about time you did. It might be better for you and everyone else."

"What are you talking about?"

"I'm talking about how your mom goes running around with different men. You think other people don't notice that? Why do you think we never hardly spent any time over at your place all these years? My folks wasn't exactly crazy about us hanging around our house all the time, you know. They just didn't want me hanging around at your house, with what was going on with your mom and all her dates."

That got my face to burning hotter than a teakettle right there. I mean, it was one thing for me to question my mom's way with men, but I sure didn't like the idea of other folks doing it. "Who my mom goes out with ain't nobody else's business."

"Well, you oughta make it your business. You know, them colleges look at more than just your football. They look at your overall reputation too. They don't want no one shining a bad light on their school."

"You saying I'm shining a bad light somehow?"

"I'm talking about that Tommy Don Clapsaddle character."

"It's Coleridge."

"Whatever. My dad told me all about him. He's bad news."

"What's supposed to be so bad about him?"

Blaine reached over and turned the radio off. "One thing is he used to play football here but turned traitor, took sides against his own team, and sold 'em out quicker than Benedict Arnold sold out to the redcoats. Ended up, he got kicked off the team and then just went totally downhill after that. My dad said he was the only hippie ever to come out of Kennisaw. Probably even sold drugs and everything else. Never did amount to any good, and now he's back sponging off his old man for a place to stay. That's about as pitiful as you can get, if you ask me. He'll probably start hitting your mom up for money. So if you don't think any of that's your business, then you ain't got the sense God gave a dog."

"How's your dad supposed to know all that?"

"How do you think? He grew up here. He knows. Just like them old boys over at the Nail. You heard what they had to say."

Blaine pulled Citronella up to the curb in front of my house. For a moment, I set there staring at the dashboard before finally opening the door.

"Hey, I'm just trying to shoot straight with you," he said.

"Okay." I didn't look at him.

"We gotta watch out for each other, don't we?"

I didn't say nothing.

"Don't we?"

"Yeah," I said finally. "That's right. We gotta watch out for each other."

Inside in the living room, I set down on our old brown couch without even turning the light on. The dim gray in there fit the way I felt good enough. It was tough to swallow the idea that the whole time last night with Tommy Don Coleridge was completely phony, but what else was I supposed to think after what Blaine and the Rusty Nail boys said?

Just about then's when I noticed a slip of paper on the coffee table. I picked it up, and for a good long while I just set there staring at the writing on the front. It was a check for a hundred dollars my mom made out to Tommy Don Coleridge. I dropped it down on the table and sank back in them couch cushions. *Blaine was right*, I thought. Tommy Don didn't waste no time hitting my mom up for money.

Seemed like she must've dropped her guard this time, somehow shook loose of that same old airtight routine she'd stuck to when it come to men. Right after my dad left, she shut herself up in her room every day after work, and I didn't even know what it was she did in there hour after hour. Then one evening, a man in a cowboy hat was setting at the kitchen table. A cowboy hat and jeans and shiny black boots. Turned out he was a welder, but he dipped snuff and talked about rodeos and riding bulls, and next thing you know, there Mom was, decked out in her own western jeans and boots and hat. For six months. Then the cowboy was gone and so was the cowboy outfits.

Next come the greenskeeper/biker, and she dressed in leathers till she threw the biker and the leathers out on the garbage heap, and then the highway patrolman and the long-haul trucker and on and on. It was just about like my real mom never come out of that back room. But this time with Tommy Don, I could've swore it was different. She seemed like her old self again—as much as I could remember what that was, anyways. I sure didn't want to see what would happen if the tables got turned, and it was Mom that got thrown over. After the way Dad done her, she probably couldn't have took it again.

It was past five o'clock in the afternoon when she come home from work, and there I was, still waiting on the couch. Now I had the lamp on, the light pointed straight down at that coffee table where I left her check for Tommy Don setting out.

"Oh, hi, honey," she said, all breezy and carefree. "I'm glad you're here. Tommy Don's having a cookout in his backyard tonight, and he said for you to come along too if you want. I think it'd be real fun to have us all there."

"*His* backyard?" I said. "Or his dad's?"

"Well, he's staying with his father right now 'cause—"

"How much is he charging for the food?"

"What? I didn't hear you." She closed the door to the hall closet after hanging her coat up.

I set forward and rested my arms on my knees. "I just want to know how much money it's gonna cost us to eat over there."

"We don't have to bring anything." She hadn't picked up on an ounce of the disgust I was putting out. "He's gonna have everything ready to go. There's gonna be grilled chicken and ears of corn and those little potatoes you like. All we have to bring is our appetites." I swear, she sounded about as happy as a kindergarten girl on paste-eating day.

I picked the check up. "Then what's this for?"

"That?" Her eyes fixed on the check. Finally, it looked like my grim old tone was sinking in. "That's just for some work he's gonna do over at the dollar store for us."

"What kind of work?"

"He's gonna paint the south wall. I'm giving him a check, and then I'll get reimbursed out of petty cash. Why? What did you think it was for?"

I looked back at the check myself, eyeballing it over like a sheriff sizing up a murder weapon. "The outside wall by Sixth Street?" I said. "That wall don't need paint."

"Not like a regular paint job. It's gonna be a mural." She was starting to sound a little wore out with me. "That's what he does. He's a painter. An artist. He paints pictures. And it was my idea. He said he'd do it for free, but I wasn't about to let him do that. Now, what's this all about?"

"*Pictures*." I just about spit the word out. Picture painting didn't sound like much of a living to a Kennisaw boy like me.

"I don't think he's the kind of guy you oughta be going out with. That's what I think."

"You what?" Her face went red. "Since when do you tell me who I ought and ought not to go out with, young man?"

Young man, she called me. Like them mothers you always hear getting on their kids over at the Wal-Mart. Only difference was my mom hadn't been around enough the last few years to start in on any *young man* business with me.

"I guess since not soon enough," I told her. "Maybe if I'd started sooner, you wouldn't have gone and got hooked up with a guy everyone else in town thinks is the biggest loser since Benedict Arnold."

"Who thinks that?" She planted her hands on her hips and gave me the squint-eye stare. "Who've you been talking to? Those numbskulls down at the Rusty Nail? Blaine's dad?"

I didn't like the way she said *Blaine's dad*, like he wasn't nothing but a stupid nobody instead of a man who once played side by side with T. Roy Strong.

"I'll tell you what," I said. "First of all, you hear enough folks say something, you figure there has to be some truth to it. And second of all, Blaine's dad's sure been around for me to talk to more than you have."

Her shoulders slumped then. The red drained right back out of her face, leaving her about as washed out as an empty bottle. "I guess I deserved that," she said. "No, I know I did."

She walked across and set next to me on the couch. It looked like she was fixing to reach over and pat my arm, but she dropped her hand back in her lap instead. "Look," she said. "I know I haven't been here for you as much as I should. I know I've been out looking for the wrong things to fill up my life. But this isn't one of those things. Tommy Don

Coleridge is a good man. Don't ask me how I know. I just feel it."

For a good long moment, I set there quiet, tapping that old check against the top of the coffee table. I didn't know the last time my mom said something to me that come straight out of her heart. Finally, I handed the check to her. "I ain't blaming you for anything," I said. "I just don't want you to get taken in by somebody 'cause he knows how to say what you want to hear."

"I don't want that to happen either."

"So, are you still gonna go over to his house tonight?"

"Yes," she said. "I am. Are you going with me?"

"No," I said. "I guess not."

CHAPTER TWENTY-TWO

Monday, I skulked back and forth past the door to the school library a good three times without going inside. After the third time, I stopped dead in the middle of the hall and flat forced myself to walk in there. I had me two real good reasons for paying a visit to the library right now, but neither one of them had the first thing to do with studying.

Reason number one had to do with Tommy Don Coleridge. I figured if he went to Kennisaw back once upon a time, then he was bound to be in a couple of the old yearbooks, and just maybe there'd be some clue in one of them about what he done to make everybody think he was such a loser.

Reason number two was every bit as important as reason number one. Sara worked the afternoon shift three times a week as a library student aide.

Ever since that stupid fight over at Wild West Days, she put her guard up anytime I got within ten yards of her, like maybe she thought I was liable to whip up another full-scale brawl just for grins. Morning, noon, and night, I kept trying to hammer out some kind of decent explanation about that durn fight, but as usual when it come to girls, I couldn't get nothing to take shape.

But now at least I had me a good reason to go into the library and talk to her. I knew how she was. If I come in asking for help, wasn't no way she'd turn me down, even if I was an idiot who got sucked into fights I didn't know the reason for fighting.

This library at our school wasn't no bigger than two classrooms put together, but she was sorting through a stack of books on a little pushcart and didn't see me come in at first. For a moment, I stood back and watched her. That famous pile of hair of hers nearly covered up her face, but that was okay. I knew them brown eyes by heart. And anyways, I liked all that hair and the way she moved, kind of herky-jerky, stoppy-starty, and the baggy way her sweatshirt and jeans fit. Comfortable and real was what she was. Not one stitch of fake anywheres on that girl.

Right when I started walking over, she looked up and pulled her hair back from her face the way she probably had to do about eight hundred thousand times a day. "Hi," she said, and maybe I was just imagining things, but her eyes looked a little bit wary—like it was a gorilla sidling up to her instead of a redheaded lunk in a black letter jacket. "Is there something you're looking for?"

You don't know how close I come to blurting out, "Yes, there is. I'm looking for *you*!" But course, I didn't do it. Instead, I told her how I wanted to look at some old yearbooks on account of I was checking out the background of a man my mom had took up with. Now, a lot of folks might've made up a story about how come they wanted to comb through old yearbooks, but like I said before, I had a hard time lying to Sara Reynolds. Which didn't mean I went into all the details about the other men that'd come and gone through my mom's life. That was one sad country song I didn't feel like singing right now.

But soon as the words dropped out of my mouth, every ounce of wary done evaporated right out of Sara's eyes, and that good old sad-soulful look filled them up again. She even admired the idea that I wanted to watch out for my mom like that. Too many kids got up into junior high and high school and quit caring about what their folks done, she said. They thought they lived in two different universes or something, but when you got right down to it, there wasn't but one universe for everyone.

I was still mulling this over while she led the way through them canyons of bookshelves to the very back of the library where the dusty volumes of Kennisaw High annuals was lined up one after another. I wasn't exactly sure how old Tommy Don Coleridge was, so we took us down several books and hauled them over to a table and started in searching.

It was a funny feeling, looking back at the faces of them students from way back when, about the same as how I felt traipsing through the dark halls of Malcolm Hickey Elementary that night I went in for Misty Koonce's trophy. Here they was, the high schoolers of Kennisaw down through the years with their different hairstyles and clothes, all the bright eyes and smiles. Kids who was grown up by now, gray in their hair and lines on their faces, kids of their own grinning in other yearbooks somewheres up on the shelf. It was a good feeling and a sad feeling both at the same time. Everything and everyone changed, and that was what always stayed the same.

"It looks like these were some pretty good times back then," Sara said.

I had to agree with that. "Yep, life looked like it was a whole lot simpler in them days."

She turned the page. "I suppose our lives would seem pretty simple too—if you just went by the pictures."

I thought of some pictures I had taken with Blaine and some of me and my mother. "I guess you're right about that."

I was enjoying setting there with Sara so much, I about forgot what we was doing, but then I spotted him. Tommy Don Coleridge in his junior year. That photo of his nearly jumped off the page. For one thing, he was probably the only boy in the whole book with long hair, but more than that, he just had a spark about him none of the others had. A real confident look in his eyes and a smile that made him seem like he was plotting up some mischief to do as soon as the camera got done clicking.

"Boy," Sara said. "He's handsome."

"You think so?"

"Kind of. If you like the type."

I wasn't much on judging handsome, but I had to admit Tommy Don probably never hurt much for dates on Saturday nights. "Maybe there's a picture of him on the football team in the back."

Sure enough, there he was in the team picture, long hair and all. And right next to him stood T. Roy Strong.

"Wait a minute here." I grabbed the yearbook and looked

at the date on the front. It was true. He never mentioned it once when he was over at our house, but he sure was. All them years back, he was right there on the greatest of the great Knights teams, a wide receiver, catching passes from T. Roy Strong hisself. There was even a separate picture of them together, along with a running back I hadn't never heard of. The caption at the bottom read "The Big Three— T. Roy Strong, Bo Early, and Tommy Don Coleridge— Kennisaw's triple threat."

"I can't believe it," I said.

"I guess he must've been pretty good."

"He must've been *real* good."

"You can't always tell a lot by that, though." Sara turned to the back of the book and started thumbing through the index to see what other high school accomplishments he had. There was a lot. Newspaper editor, Latin club president, student council, National Honor Society, art club, basketball, baseball. They even had a picture of him wearing these raggedy overalls for a comical skit in a school hootenanny, a big giant cowboy hat cocked up on his head and a corncob pipe stuck in his teeth.

"Wow," Sara said. "Unless he's changed since then, it looks like your mom might've found herself a real good guy."

"I guess." It did seem that way, all right, but something didn't add up. Why would Blaine's dad and the Rusty Nail boys have such low opinions of a guy like we was looking at here?

"She's lucky." Sara stared down at the hootenanny picture. "It looks like she's got two real good guys in her life."

"No," I said. "Just one. She ain't seeing that car-lot guy no more."

She laughed. "I was talking about *you*. You're the other good guy in her life. I mean, going to this much trouble to watch out for her and all."

"Oh." I looked down and rubbed my hand across the short bristles on top of my head.

"It's just kind of hard to figure. I mean, the way you are now and the way you are in class and that night we went over to the café to study, and then how you were at the park. One second we were just talking away, and then the next second, you're in the middle of a fight with boys you didn't even know."

There it was. I knew it was bound to come up, but all I could think to say was, "I can't figure it neither. I ain't usually like that. It just started happening so fast."

"I like you this way a lot better." She looked at me through a couple loose strands of hair, and it seemed like maybe she was trying to figure whuther I was glad she felt like that or not.

"Well," I said before I could think too much and throw myself off. "You know, if you wanted to go do something sometime, I could pretty much guarantee you I wouldn't get in a fight this time."

She gave it a little bitty smile then. "I'd like that."

"You know what I was thinking?" I charged right on ahead. "I was thinking about how you said you'd like to take a walk out in the country like we was talking about over there at Sweet's that time, and so I figured maybe we could do that this Saturday."

"Saturday?" Them little fingers of hers traced a nervous squiggly line on the tabletop. "I thought you'd be celebrating winning your last big game on Saturday."

"Naw," I said. "I'd ruther do this. We could get up early to watch the sun come up and bring us along a picnic and everything if it's not too cold. I'll show you my favorite spot."

"I think it's supposed to be real nice this weekend, good and warm."

"So, you want to go? I'll borrow my mom's car."

"I'd love to," she said.

I couldn't believe it was so easy. Here we was setting side by side, talking about going out together as natural as grass growing. Nothing awkward about it. Course, the first instinct I had was to run out of there before something went wrong, but at the same time I could've gone on setting with her till winter come. Or at least till the janitor showed up and run us out.

"You know what?" I said. "Maybe we oughta look at his senior yearbook too."

"That's a good idea." She had her a big smile like she was thinking she wasn't in no hurry to get done neither.

The senior yearbook was the next one on the stack, and this time I turned straight back to the football pictures. Same as before, Tommy Don and T. Roy stood there shoulder to shoulder, but this time Tommy Don didn't show up in one single other picture in that whole football section, and they had them a *lot* of football pictures in there too. That didn't necessarily mean nothing, and I sure ain't no detective, but what I found next seemed pretty strange.

"Look at this here," I said, pointing to a photo that took up nearly half a page. "It's a picture of the team the night they won state. They got the trophy setting out in front, and everyone's there, except Tommy Don Coleridge. Where's he? Why wouldn't he be in that picture?"

"I don't know."

"I think I do. I think he got kicked off the team for something. Something they don't put in yearbooks." I went on and explained what all I'd heard off Blaine and the Rusty Nail gang, but she didn't think that proved nothing.

"Sounds to me like you need to talk to Tommy Don about it," she said. "Hear his side."

"You mean just go over there and ask him straight out?"

"Why not? It'd sure be a lot better than going on what Blaine Keller said."

There it went. The mood in the room changed about as fast as if someone flipped a switch on it. "Why's that?" I said, leaning away from her so's I could get a better view of what she was fixing to say. "It's not like Blaine's got any reason to make things up on Tommy Don."

"Well, I just don't know if Blaine's the best one to listen to." She had a look in her eyes that reminded me of how a teacher will look at you when they're fixing to explain why the answer you just gave didn't have an ounce of right to it—front, back, or center. "After all, he's the one that got you in that fight."

"Hey," I said. "Blaine would back me up if I got in a fight. That's what buddies do."

"But I witnessed the whole thing." Now she sounded like a teacher too. "Blaine just walked right up and punched that boy without so much as saying hello, and then it was like he went insane. What are you going to do, get in a brawl every time Blaine Keller feels like hitting someone for no reason?"

Boy howdy. I wouldn't have thought I could get mad at Sara, but this was hard to take. With all the deep ideas she had, it was hard to figure how she could be so dense about this. "Look," I said, staring down at the stack of yearbooks. "You wouldn't understand how it is with good buddies like me and Blaine."

"Understand what? That you let Blaine do all your thinking for you?"

I took me a deep breath on that one, trying to stay calm. "I'm talking about loyalty," I said. "Sticking by the folks who's on your side. You don't go around asking questions about that. You just do it before it's too late."

"Well, that's dumb. If you don't ask questions you could end up doing all sorts of things. How do you think the Nazis kept going?"

Nazis. You got to hate it when someone brings the Nazis in on you.

The overhead lights glared down on that picture of the championship team without Tommy Don Coleridge. *Damn*, I thought. *This is what you get when two people go to trying to open up to each other. You end up seeing sides of them you didn't never want to see.*

"You know what?" I said just barely loud enough for her to hear me. "Maybe we oughta forget about Saturday."

"What?"

"If you think I'm so dumb, maybe you oughta see if you can't get someone else to take you on a picnic."

"That's not what I meant." She put her hand on my arm, but I pulled away and shut the yearbook.

"Look," I said. "There's Benjamin Deal up there at the checkout desk." Benjamin Deal was a sophomore, probably no more than five foot tall, with a big head. He was the only kid I knew that carried a handkerchief. "I'll bet old Benjamin would take you out any day of the week."

"Benjamin Deal? What are you talking about? I don't want to go anywhere with Benjamin Deal."

"Why not? He's a brain. You two'd be perfect together. You stick with your kind, and I'll stick with my kind."

"My *kind?*" She set back in her seat and eyed me over like she was fixing to sentence me down to detention hall. "Now you do sound dumb."

"That's okay. Maybe that's just who I am." I stood up from the table. "Thanks for the help."

She stood up too. "Wait a minute, Hampton. Let's talk about this."

"That's all right," I said, turning away. "We talked too much already."

CHAPTER TWENTY-THREE

At home after football practice, my gut was still burning over that argument with Sara. She didn't know Blaine like I did. She didn't know what all we went through together, how Blaine and his dad treated me like family when I didn't feel like I had much of one. The way I figured it, girls just didn't understand loyalty, plain and simple. And I wasn't the only one that had to learn it the hard way. Blaine just found it out hisself too. Big-time.

He gave me the story on the whole shooting match in blow-by-blow detail. What happened was, after we left the Rusty Nail last Saturday, he bought him a six-pack on top of what he already drunk at the Nail. Around six or so, he picked up Rachel, and they hadn't no more started cruising the drag when they broke into a fight. It might not have been World War III right then, but it was building up to it.

First he got on her about spending too much time around Don Manly up at the furniture store, and then she come back at him for drinking too much, but the last straw dropped when they run across the Pawtuska boys.

They was in the middle of Main when Rachel jammed her hands up against the dashboard and hollered, "Watch out! You almost hit that guy's bumper in front of us!"

So what did Blaine do? He just pumped the brake and let out a nasty laugh and said, "So what? Why's this truck in our town anyways? Probably some fool from Okalah coming in here to spy on us for the game Friday."

Rachel told him she knew for a fact them boys up there wasn't from Okalah, they was from Pawtuska, and that didn't set too well with Blaine neither.

"How do you know that?" he said. "You hanging around with Pawtuska boys now?"

"I'm not hanging around with 'em," she told him. "I just know who the one driving is. Misty dated him a couple of times."

So that got Blaine disgusted with Misty. "I don't know why you hang out with that girl," he said. "If her dad didn't have money, she'd just be a plain tramp."

Now Citronella edged up almost within grinding distance of the Pawtuska boys' bumper before Blaine backed off at the last second. Then at the stoplight, he pulled up next to them, squeezing into this real narrow space between the truck and curb. There was three of them up there in the cab, and the one on the passenger side rolled down his window and said, "Hey, dumbass, what's the idea of tailgating us?"

Blaine eyed him over and said, " 'Cause I don't like fools from Okalah on our drag, that's what."

The one in the middle hollered, "We ain't from Okalah. We're from Pawtuska."

"Told you," Rachel said, but Blaine didn't pay no attention to her.

"Well, I wouldn't sound so proud of it if I was you," he said.

The one on the passenger side looked Citronella up and down. "Well, if I was you, I wouldn't be talking, driving around in a piece of crap like that."

Just then, the light changed, and the Pawtuska boys drove off, laughing. You better believe Blaine was hotter than a spark plug on that. He pulled in right behind that truck again, only this time he got too close, and Citronella jolted against their bumper, not hard enough to cause a wreck, but plenty hard enough to mash in a dent about the size of a gravy dish back there.

That got Rachel to damning him to hell worse than a preacher at a tent revival meeting, but he didn't do nothing but laugh at her, and when them Pawtuska boys turned into the Wal-Mart parking lot, he pulled in right after them.

Trouble was, them boys piled out of that truck armed to the teeth with monkey wrenches and baseball bats. Blaine took a quick look around the parking lot to see if he might have him some allies hanging around like kids do on a Saturday night, but this early in the evening there wasn't nothing but a crew of girls setting on the hood of Darla Monroe's Camaro.

Rachel started screaming for him to get the hell out of there, but she ought to have known Blaine better than that.

"If this is the way you want it," he said, gunning his engine, "then, boys, this is the way you're gonna get it."

Rachel braced her hand against the dashboard again. "What are you doing? Are you crazy?"

He didn't even answer. He just threw the shifter into gear,

stomped on the gas, and yelled out the window, "Fill your hands, you sonofabitch!" Which, if you don't know, is what John Wayne yells in *True Grit*, riding off to do battle with a patch on his eye.

Old Citronella fishtailed across the pavement straight at them three boys from Pawtuska, and they took to scattering, but not before one of them flung his baseball bat hard as he could. It bounced once off the hood, then smacked a hard one into the windshield. Luckily, it didn't bust through but went rattling away off the roof.

Rachel went off like a homemade firecracker then. "You idiot! That bat could've broke clean through the window and killed me dead."

But Blaine just said, "What are you yelling at me for? I didn't throw it." Which was true, but Rachel didn't think that was the point and went to screaming for him to drive her home before they both did get killed.

Blaine wasn't about to drive nobody home, though. Instead, he just turned Citronella around, glared through that cracked windshield, and revved the engine. This time them Pawtuska boys scurried back to their truck and climbed in faster than a pack of squirrels into a knothole.

"Running ain't gonna save you boys," Blaine said.

Inside the pickup, the driver was fumbling with his keys, a look on his face like he seen the shadow of God fixing to smite him down. Blaine revved the engine again and grabbed the shifter, but before he could tromp on the gas, Rachel yanked the keys out of the ignition and jammed them behind her back. Meantime, across the parking lot, the Pawtuska boys' pickup peeled away, hands flipping the bird out of the windows on both sides.

"I don't know what's got into you anymore," Rachel said, still holding the keys behind her. "But I'm about fed up."

Blaine just gripped on to the steering wheel, watching that pickup truck's taillights disappear down the road. "Give me my keys," was all he said.

She didn't budge. "You keep on acting like this and someone's gonna get hurt, and I'll tell you what, I sure don't want it to be me."

"Darla Monroe and all her friends are over there staring at us," Blaine said, not yelling or anything, keeping as under control as he could. "I don't want them thinking even my own girlfriend's turning against me."

Rachel done made her mind up to have it out, though. "Don't pull that old routine on me. Just because I don't go along with everything you want to do doesn't mean I'm turning against you."

That right there was Blaine's idea of loyalty, though, and he let her know it too. "You can bet if my buddies was here they wouldn't be yelling, 'Let me out, let me out,' and grabbing my keys away from me."

Rachel just gave him a snort and said, "You say that like they'd be doing you a favor, but you know what? One of these days I'm not gonna be around, and you're gonna get yourself in some real trouble you can't get out of."

"Look," Blaine said. "Darla's walking over here. Go on and give me my keys right now."

She glanced at Darla and then turned back to Blaine. "Can't you at least talk to me about what's bugging you?"

Blaine held out his hand and said, "Nothing's bugging me. Now you gonna give me my keys or am I gonna have to ride home with Darla?"

He got her with that one. "I give up," she said, and dropped the keys in his palm. "If anyone's riding home with Darla, it's gonna be me. You can go drive yourself off a cliff, for all I care."

Blaine wasn't playing no games with her, though. "If you walk off from here, don't think you're gonna call me up crying about getting back together."

"You can forget that," she said. "I don't even want to hear your voice unless you're down on your knees apologizing."

He started to tell her not to hold her breath on that, but she slammed the door before he finished. And that was it. They hadn't spoke a word to each other since that night.

When he finished off telling me the story, he said he had one piece of advice that I ought to learn right now. "Don't never apologize to a girl," he said. "They'll think they own you if you do. You can bet the sun'll burn out into a cold black cinder before Rachel gets an apology out of me."

Well, I didn't have no apologies in mind to give at the moment neither. No girl was going to think she owned me. I told myself that over and over. But somehow it didn't make me feel no better.

CHAPTER TWENTY-FOUR

I still thought Sara was one hundred percent wrong about standing by your buddies, but I did have to admit she was right about something else. I ought to go over to Tommy Don Coleridge's house and talk to him face to face. A man at least deserved a chance to tell his side of things.

The Kennisaw phone book only listed one Coleridge, so I didn't have no problem finding the right house. That was another thing that bugged me, a man Tommy Don's age living with his daddy. Sponging off him. That'd take a lot of explaining right off the bat. I rang the doorbell, but no one answered, so I knocked a couple times, not real hard, just loud enough to show I at least gave it a good try. I was about to call it quits when the door opened, and there Tommy Don stood, a paintbrush in one hand and paint spatters up and down his jeans and sweater.

"Hampton," he said, breaking into that big wide grin of his. "I didn't expect to see you here. Come on in. It's a little chilly out there tonight."

"It ain't bad," I said, stepping inside. All the sudden, I was a little more nervous than I thought I'd be.

Tommy Don suggested we ought to go on out to the garage and talk. His father was resting in the other room, and he didn't want to disturb him.

"I was just finishing up some work out here," he said, shutting the door to the garage behind us. "Have you a seat on the wooden bench over there. Sorry to have to bring you out here, but Dad hasn't been doing real well."

There wasn't no reason to apologize about the garage. It had a good comfortable feel to it. Every corner and every shelf was filled up with the kind of stuff you'd accumulate over a long life. Old clocks, lamps, fishing tackle, scuffed-up trunks, and just about every kind of tool you could think of. Outside the side window, there was a half-moon shining in and the bushy silhouette of an evergreen tree pressing against the glass.

What Mom said about Tommy Don being a picture painter turned out to be true. He had him an easel set up by the back wall, and there was a good paint smell hanging in the air. For a second, he stood on the other side of the easel, I guess sizing up the painting there, but it was facing the other way, so I couldn't see what it was.

"Cancer," Tommy Don said.

"Pardon me?"

"My father needs his rest because he's been fighting cancer. Started in his prostate, but it seems like it's spreading everywhere now. That's why I moved in here with him. I want him to be able to stay in his own home for as long as possible."

"Oh," I said. That took care of one explanation, and I got to admit I felt a pretty good-size shot of guilt over thinking he wasn't doing nothing but sponging. "Where was you living before this?"

Tommy Don took note of something on the canvas, dabbed at it with his paintbrush, and then nodded, satisfied with whatever it was he done. "Santa Fe," he said. "I still have a studio out there." He set the paintbrush down, pulled up an old-fashioned metal lawn chair, and took a seat.

"So, Hampton, what brings you over here today?" The painting was forgot then, and he had all his attention tuned in towards me.

I didn't know much where to start, though. I was still a little thrown off, first by finding out about his dad's cancer and then just by the comfortable way Tommy Don acted. It was hard to believe anyone like that had a rotten past to him. "Umm," I said like a fool. "Uh. So. Santa Fe, huh? I guess that's a pretty long ways away."

"Not that far. You can drive it in a day if you have to. I know, I've done it. Texas panhandle isn't much to look at, but when you get into New Mexico, there's just something about the landscape out there. It's spiritual."

Now, I didn't know many folks likely to use the word *spiritual* outside of church deals, but I had heard someone else say it not too long ago. Sara. We was talking about how the land looked then too.

"I guess I know what you're thinking," Tommy Don said. "You're wondering where your mom fits into that."

That wasn't exactly what I was thinking, but now that he brought it up, I figured it was a pretty important point.

"I don't blame you for being concerned," he went on. "My

mom passed on quite a while back, and I've tried to do what I can for my dad. That's what family's for."

"My dad run off on us," I said, which surprised even me. It wasn't something I said out loud in front of too many people.

"I know it," Tommy Don said, and he had a look in his eyes like it really hurt him to think about that happening to me. "Your mom told me about that. It's a tough thing. I wouldn't be surprised if the two of you didn't go around thinking that was a reflection on you, but it's not. That was him. He didn't know what he had. I'll guarantee you that. But some men don't know who they are, so how can they know what they want?"

There he went, reminding me of Sara again. Made me wonder if maybe there wasn't more folks out in the world that I could talk to about things like that than I ever thought there was.

"I don't know if my mom knows what she wants neither," I said.

"You might be surprised about her. Have you ever read any of her poetry?"

"Poetry? My mom writes poetry?"

"She does for a fact."

That was just like her, I thought. Up to her old tricks. If Tommy Don was an artist, then she'd be artistic herself and whip out some poetry to get in good with him. But then I remembered something, just a scrap of an old memory from the days before my dad run off. I was so little, me and her could lay there on the couch with me in front and her arms around me. She held out this yellow notepad filled up with her own handwriting and little drawings, and she read off page after page out loud. It was almost like music.

"I told her," Tommy Don went on, "she oughta send her poetry off to one of those literary journals. It's some of the most incredible I ever read. Like Emily Dickinson, only with more real-life experience."

That impressed me right there. I had to read me some Emily Dickinson poems sophomore year. They was weird, but I liked a few of them pretty good. Not that I would've told no one that.

"See," Tommy Don said. "She doesn't know what she's got. She has all these things inside her that she's afraid to show to anyone because one man couldn't see it in her."

I knew a lot more than one man didn't never see what she had in her, the latest one being old Jim Houck, the hotshot from Lowery, but what Tommy Don said made sense. I sure understood how it was being around folks you couldn't show things to.

"But"—Tommy Don leaned back in his chair—"I guess all that doesn't answer the question of what happens when the time comes for me to head back to Santa Fe."

"No, sir," I said. "It don't answer that one."

"And the bad thing is, I don't know what answer to give you. Too early to tell. But sometimes you have to take your chances."

I stared at that clean-swept garage floor, remembering the time I come home to find Mom out on the front porch, the tear tracks down her cheeks. What would happen this time if someone she opened herself up to—someone who could see everything inside her—picked up and drove away? If that was Tommy Don's idea of taking chances, I didn't want no part of it. The way I seen it, you chose your side and you stuck to it, no matter what. That's what loyalty was. But then, I guessed maybe that was why Tommy Don had the bad reputation he had.

"There's something else I wanted to ask you," I said, trying to work up the courage to come out with it.

"Ask me anything you want to," Tommy Don said, smiling.

"Well," I said. "It's just I was kind of wondering what happened to you on the football team back in high school."

"What do you mean?"

I hated sounding like I was accusing him of something, but there wasn't no way around it. "The thing is, I heard you got kicked off the team."

His smile come undone around the edges on that. "Who told you that?"

"A lot of folks." I tried to think up the most reliable names. "Haywood Ritter. My best friend Blaine Keller's dad."

"Old Haywood and little Frankie Keller, huh?" The smile sort of inched back, but it looked a touch sour this time.

"They said you took sides against your own team."

"Well, I guess I remember it a little different than they do."

"Something must've happened." I was in the middle of it now and kept on talking even though I wasn't real sure where I was headed. "I looked you up in an old yearbook, and you was in there with the team picture, and then there was another one with you and T. Roy Strong and another guy, Bo somebody. But then you wasn't in the picture at the state championship. There ain't nobody wouldn't show up for that picture unless something pretty bad happened."

Tommy Don nodded, his eyes narrowed down. "You really did some detective work, didn't you? That's good. I'm proud of you for wanting to protect your mom that way. That tells me a lot about you and your character."

"That's okay," I said. "But it still don't mean Mr. Keller or Mr. Ritter was wrong about what happened."

"No, it doesn't." Tommy Don rubbed at his chin. He was

177

all serious now. "But it seems like to me you have your suspicions or you wouldn't come ask my side of it. That takes integrity right there. It means you're asking questions for yourself instead of taking the word of a couple of folks who didn't even play on the team."

"Mr. Keller played on the team," I cut in. "Blaine told me. He played right alongside T. Roy Strong his last year."

Tommy Don shook his head. "Frankie Keller was three years younger than us, and he was the equipment manager. Go back and look at the yearbook again if you don't believe me. But I don't care if he goes around telling people he played for the Dallas Cowboys. He can say he scored forty touchdowns in the Super Bowl if he wants to, but as for what I did, I'd just as soon tell my side of it myself."

He stopped and looked out the window for a second, I guess gathering up the past into a story. "First off, I loved Kennisaw football. Loved it. We were a phenomenal team too. Five undefeated seasons in a row, and I played for three of those seasons. Well, two and a half. And old T. Roy was a great player. He was beautiful to watch on the field, no doubt about it. But he wasn't the best player on the team."

My eyes must've about half bugged out of my head when I heard that.

"I know it's hard to believe," Tommy Don went on. "T. Roy with his state records and his Super Bowl rings—they'll never stop telling tales about him. And don't get me wrong, I liked T. Roy. We were tight. You should've seen us. We about ran these old hills ragged. But Bo Early was the real best player on the team. Man, could that guy run. You might as well've tried to tackle the wind. They used to tell a story around here—maybe they still do—about T. Roy throwing a

178

touchdown pass for a hundred and nine yards and thirty-five inches or something like that. Problem is, that never happened. What really happened was Bo Early took a pitch in the back of the end zone and ran that far for a touchdown. I was there. It was the most glorious thing I ever saw. But they stopped telling stories about old Bo a long time ago."

"How come?" I was so caught up in the story, I about forgot why I come over in the first place.

"Let me ask you this." Tommy Don leaned forward. "How many black kids do you have on your team?"

"I don't know," I said. "I never set down and counted 'em. You mean including juniors and sophomores?"

"That's just my point. You have quite a few, enough that you don't even bother to keep track. But when I was in school here, there was only one black kid in the whole school, Bo Early. I guess you didn't notice that when you were looking through the yearbook."

"I guess not."

"It was a lot different back then. The guys on the team liked him all right, and they loved the way he played, but they didn't hang out with him when practice was over. He had two friends in the entire school, me and T. Roy Strong. Of course, no one ever tried to give T. Roy a hard time about it, just because of who he was, but some of 'em said some pretty harsh things to me. Not a lot—everyone thought I was pretty crazy anyway—but enough to know there were some ugly ideas floating around."

I caught myself clenching my fists, thinking about someone pulling that kind of stuff on me about hanging out with Darnell or any of the other black guys I hung out with. "I'll tell you what," I said. "I'd sure give some fools a good piece of my mind if they tried telling me not to hang out with my buddies."

"Even if they were your own teammates, good old Kennisaw Knights just like you?"

"None of my teammates'd say nothing like that." And it was true. No one would have told me I shouldn't be friends with Darnell. But on the other hand—if I wanted to be honest with myself—I had to admit there was times when some of the white boys would be setting around, maybe drinking some beers, and jokes got told or words got used I sure wouldn't want any of my black friends to hear. And I never spoke up the way I should have.

"Maybe they wouldn't," Tommy Don said. "Maybe it'd be something else, something you don't even hardly notice at first. But back then that was how most folks thought, even the grown-ups. Especially the grown-ups. But Bo was so good at football everyone in town was nice to him. To his face, anyway. And I'll tell you what, it would've been him breaking all the state records our senior year if it hadn't been for what happened that one day out in Leonard Biggins Park.

"There Bo was, sitting on a picnic table with Amanda Cox." Tommy Don smiled. "Amanda Cox—whew!—that girl was something else. Grown men just about wrecked their pickup trucks when she walked down Main Street. But she was white as the inside of an apple, and back then if you were black, you just didn't go around sitting on picnic tables with the likes of blond-haired, blue-eyed Amanda Cox. Not in Kennisaw. Of course, she was enjoying it every bit as much as Bo, but here came three guys from the team, ready to start up trouble. They weren't even good enough to tie the laces on Bo's cleats, but they laid into him with a buncha bull about how he oughta know his place. Big mistake. Bo wasn't the type to sit still for anyone telling him what his place was. Now, there being three of them and just one of Bo, they got the better of him in the end, but I guarantee they didn't look as much like they won a fight as like they just got spit out of the wrong end of a cement mixer.

"That wasn't the end of it, though. At the next practice, word got going around about Bo and Amanda, rumors saying a lot more went on between them than really did, and how Bo had the audacity to fight back when the others came over to stand up for her honor. As if those idiots cared about any girl's honor with the way they were always lying about their own girlfriends.

"Anyway, we were setting up to run the offense, and Coach calls Bo's number. T. Roy handed off to him as smooth as ever, but right then the offensive line just stood up and put their hands on their hips and let the defense rumble in and pile all over Bo like an avalanche crashing down. I don't think T. Roy knew about if beforehand. I know I sure didn't, but Coach had to know because he didn't say a word to anyone about it. Just blew his whistle and told us to line back up, called Bo's number again, and it was the same thing. The offense stood there and let Bo get slaughtered.

"I asked Coach if he wasn't gonna do something, but he just told me to shut up and take my position. So for the third time, he called Bo's number, and the line let the defense in like before, everyone stampeding at Bo, the whole team piling on, arms and legs flying everywhere. And then after about ten seconds, here came Bo, bulling his way out the other side of that pile, and no one could catch him then.

"Coach blew his whistle till he got red in the face, but old

Bo just kept on running clear to the end zone, and when he got there, he turned around and set the ball down as calm as could be and walked off the field. When I saw that, I knew what I had to do. I didn't even have to think it over. I just took my helmet off too and walked right after him. Coach hollered and hollered, ordering me to get back to my position or not come back at all, but I kept on walking."

"What'd T. Roy do?" I asked, even though I pretty much knew what the answer had to be.

Tommy Don leaned back in his chair. "T. Roy? He stayed. I looked at him as I passed by and asked him if he was coming with us, but he just shook his head. We didn't run together much after that, and I never played for the Knights again."

"And Bo Early? Did that pretty much end his chances right there?" For some reason, I expected he probably ended up living in a cardboard box down under the railroad trestle, but that wasn't how it turned out.

"Well," Tommy Don said. "He didn't play any more high school ball, but he did play in college while he was earning his degree. He's an attorney in Tulsa now. A good one too."

I looked down at the hard gray floor. "No one ever told me that side of it."

"No." Tommy Don cocked his head. "I didn't figure they did. That's how it is with legends. The greater they sound, the more must've got left out."

That was something I had to save and think about another time. It was getting late, and all the sudden, I was real tired. Old Samson in the Bible story probably felt about the same way after his haircut. "I appreciate you talking to me," I said, making sure to look Tommy Don in the eye. "I had a friend of mine tell me there might be another side to what I got told, and I guess she was right. You cleared some things up for me."

I stood up and Tommy Don did too.

"I'm glad you came over," he said. "Maybe you could do me a favor before you take off. I've been working on this painting all afternoon, trying to get the right feel to it. Maybe you could take a look at it and tell me what you think."

"I don't know much about painting," I said. "But I'll give her a look-see."

At first, I couldn't tell what in the world it was supposed to be. The whole painting seemed like it wasn't nothing but a mishmash of colors changing from a kind of blue-black up top to purple to red to gold and then down to bronze. Truth be told, I didn't know what to say, so I just stood there gawking till a strange thing happened. That painting seemed to reach out and yank me right into it. There I stood, smack in the middle of them colors, and I realized what they was. The different shades of the sky at sunset, leading down to the ground. And I swear, I could smell the earth and hear the breeze and feel the cool of the evening coming on. Stars would be wheeling out soon and then the moon would circle over and change the colors of everything.

"It's spiritual," I said.

Tommy Don put his hand on my shoulder. "Thanks. That's what I was trying for."

"That's the first painting I ever looked at," I said. "I mean *really* looked at."

"Well, if you want to talk painting some, you're welcome to stay on awhile. I'm always looking for someone who understands what I'm trying to do with 'em."

"Thanks," I said, reaching out to shake his hand. "I'd sure like to, but there's somewheres else I have to stop off before I head home. I think I got some apologizing to do."

CHAPTER TWENTY-FIVE

That old Kennisaw High gym was packed to the rafters, sophomores up in their section, the juniors over in theirs, and then the seniors closest to where the football team set. With the seats filled, most of the teachers stood around on the floor underneath this big long banner that told us to go out and make history tonight.

After Coach Huff finished off his pep talk, I was next in line. The microphone there at the scuffed wood lectern was too low, so I had to lean way over to speak into it. Usually, I hated talking at pep rallies more than about anything, but this time I knew exactly what I wanted to say.

"Tonight, we have us a chance to do something not too many teams ever get to even try for." My voice come out soft and a little muffled from leaning in too close to the mike, so

I paused for a second and then tried raising the volume up a notch. "And I'm here to say right now we better finish off our work quick 'cause I got plans to jump up out of bed early tomorrow morning and go for a long, long walk in the country."

For a second, the crowd waited—I guess they wasn't sure whuther I was finished or not—but when I stepped back away from the lectern, they busted loose with a good-size cheer, just like they knew what I was talking about. Me, I looked up into the top of the senior section and smiled. I done already picked out where Sara was.

Turned out, apologizing to her was one of the easiest things I ever done. All the explanations I run through my head on the way over to her place from Tommy Don's didn't matter worth a day-old donut. When I got there, she come out on the front porch and we stood over by her dad's wheelchair ramp, and all I said was, "I'm sorry."

She didn't make me feel ten different kinds of bad before making up neither. And she sure didn't start acting like she owned me the way Blaine said. She just shined them brown eyes on me and said, "I'm sorry too," and invited me to come inside.

We must've talked for an hour in that converted-garage library of theirs. Some guys, if they'd been setting close to a girl like I was, they'd have probably started in on the kissing and wrestling, but that wasn't my style. Nothing against them guys, but I realized I had me my own pace. Maybe I should've been born in a different time. One thing I do know, though, when I walked home that night, I sure didn't have the feeling anymore like I was a tree that fell down in the forest with no one around to hear it.

Darnell was the next one up at the lectern and he gave it a deep, smooth voice almost like a disc jockey or something. "We're gonna get it done in the first quarter," he said. "We're gonna get it done in the second quarter. And you better believe we're gonna get it done in the third quarter. And then in the fourth quarter, we're gonna come back and do it all over again!" He punched his fist up in the air. "Fight 'em, Knights!"

The cheers busted loose again, growing louder and louder as Blaine walked up to take his turn. He was always dramatic about it when he got up there. He adjusted the microphone for his height and tapped at it to make sure the sound was right. For a good long moment, he stared into the stands, moving his eyes from section to section, pulling everyone in with his dead-serious glare. Finally, the cheers simmered down.

"Tonight, we ain't just playing a game," he started. "Games are for children. This is war!"

There went the cheers again.

He waited them out, then started back in. "Tonight, the Knights'll be more than just a football team. For a lot of years, our town's had a reputation and tradition that's burned as bright as a torch on a cold, dark night. We're the keepers of that flame, and we mean to light up these hills with it!"

That one got the crowd more juiced up than ever, yelling and clapping and stomping their feet on the bleachers, making that loud, low rumble that gets you right in the stomach.

"Before coming here today," Blaine went on when the noise faded off, "I looked up the word *knight* in the dictionary, and do you know what it said? It said that knights are gentlemen, nobility, raised to honorable military rank, soldiers trained to fight for their country. And that's our patriotic duty tonight. Our enemy's the worst kind of enemy, a team without honor. They might share these same hills with us, all right, but they sure don't share our traditions. Almost thirty years ago, an Okalah team cheated their way to ending the greatest string of wins any hill-country team ever put together, and they had to wait till the great T. Roy Strong graduated to do it. Are we gonna let 'em do it a second time?"

"No!" the crowd roared.

"Are we?"

"No!"

"That's right. Tonight, when we go on that field as the Kennisaw Knights, noble soldiers and carriers of the honor and dignity of our school and our whole town, I'll promise you this, by God, we're gonna stomp the Okalah Outlaws into the ground or we're gonna die trying!"

All at once, the crowd jumped up to its feet, the cheers bouncing off the walls and the ceiling, and the bleachers rumbling from stomping feet. You could practically see how the noise was swelling up inside of Blaine as he raised his fists in the air. He meant what he said. I believed that. He would die trying, if that's what it took.

CHAPTER TWENTY-SIX

After the pep assembly, Coach caught me by the arm and told me to come over to his office, said he had something to talk over just between me and him. Blaine heard him and asked me what was up.

"I don't have any idea," I said. "As far as I know, I haven't done anything wrong."

"Seems kinda strange." Blaine looked suspicious. "Wonder why he didn't ask me to come over too."

That was a good point, Blaine being offensive captain and all. "Maybe he just wants to go over some last-minute defense stuff," I said.

"Maybe." Blaine didn't look too sure about that. It wasn't like Coach to talk his ideas over with you. He just told you what to do and you did it. "Or maybe he didn't like that little speech you gave. I mean, what were you talking about?"

"Aw, surely he didn't care about that. He knows I'm not much on public speaking. Anyways, I better get over there. I'll fill you in on it later."

"Yeah, you do that."

I always felt out of place in Coach's office. Everything was so shiny and neat, and then there was me. I felt like I ought to go get my clothes ironed or something. He never was one of them coaches you hear about that asks his players over to his house or takes them out to the lake and feeds them on catfish and watermelon. You didn't come into his office and lay out your personal problems. He was all business all the time. Except today, he had a little more friendly to him.

First thing when I walked in, he went over and shut the door, and on his way back to his desk he told me to set down and slapped me a warm pat on the back.

"How'd you sleep last night?" he said.

"Pretty good."

"That's fine. We need you in top form tonight." He leaned back in his chair and made a little tent with his fingers in front of his stomach. "But that's not really what I called you in here for."

"Well," I said, "if it's about that little speech I made, I'm sorry it didn't make a whole lot of sense. . . ."

He chuckled. "No, Hampton, that's not what it's about." When he called me Hampton instead of Green, I knew he had something different from the usual game talk on his mind.

"It's a heck of a lot more important than that," he went on. "You know how I sent off that game film to OU? Well, I got some word back about that. Nothing official, now, but still real, real reliable."

That sure got my attention.

"And I'll just tell you this. They liked what they saw. They liked what they saw a whole lot."

"Well," I said, "we played some good ball this season. I'll bet our team could whup plenty of those 6A boys."

"It's not the team I'm talking about." Coach leaned forward and stared me in the eye. "It's you, Hampton. You impressed the hell out of some important people. And I wouldn't say this if I wasn't pretty certain, but things look real good for you at OU. Signing day's still a couple months off, but things look real promising."

"Just me?" I asked. "They didn't say nothing about anyone else?"

"There isn't anyone else to talk about. We're a hell of a 4A team, Hampton. A hell of a 4A team. But unless someone really steps up huge here at the end of the season, I don't see anybody but you having much of a chance with any big-time college programs."

I didn't know what to say to that—Coach didn't pass out compliments too much. But more than that, I didn't know how to *feel*. One part of me felt like jumping up on the desk and shouting *hurray*! But another part felt real let down. Football hadn't never been just about me. It was about the rest of the guys on the team too. And especially Blaine.

"So," Coach went on, "the reason I'm telling you this right now is so you'll get out there tonight and play—not just like a 4A hotshot—but like the OU-caliber linebacker you are. You got that?"

"You bet, Coach."

"All right, then." He got up and come around the desk and shook my hand. "Finish off this game proud for us, son."

When I come out of the office, Blaine was down by the

water fountain, pretending to get a drink. He wiped his mouth with his forearm. "Well, what did he have on his mind?"

"Oh, nothing much." I couldn't look him in the eye.

He stood there and studied me for a moment. "It was about OU, wasn't it? Coach heard back about that game film."

I never did have much of a poker face.

"Nothing official," I said. "Just that they kind of liked it."

"You mean they liked *you*."

I didn't say anything.

"Good for you," he said, but there wasn't much enthusiasm in it. "That's great."

"Coach said there was still time for someone to step up and maybe make a big impression."

Blaine started walking. "I ain't even worried about that. Five undefeated seasons—that's all I got on my mind, son. Five undefeated seasons. There ain't nothing bigger than that."

CHAPTER TWENTY-SEVEN

There we was, under the lights again. A constant roar filled up the stadium. I bowled over two blockers, dodged a third one, and hammered into that Okalah tailback so hard I could just about feel the wind whooshing out of him. Five-yard loss. Okalah had to give up the ball. Again.

But Blaine was wrong. It *was* a game.

Or if you had to say it was something more than that, then it wasn't no war. Huh-uh. It was a song you could belt out at the top of your lungs, letting loose everything you kept inside and didn't know how to get out any other way. Whatever it was, I knew one thing for sure. I was having me more fun playing football than any time since grade school days.

"What're you smiling at?" Blaine yelled when I pulled my helmet off on the sideline. "We gotta get intense, son!"

I slapped him a good one on the back. "I am intense!"

Blaine tugged his own helmet down over his ears. "You better wipe that goofy-ass grin off your face before you fool around and lose us this game."

I just laughed. I wasn't worried one bit. The more fun I had, the better I played. That whole first half I was all over the field, racking up one tackle after the other. Two pass deflections, four sacks, and one interception. Boy howdy. I hadn't never had a game to match this one.

That good old Kennisaw crowd went crazy with just about everything I done. I probably could've tied my shoe and they would've started chanting my name. Paper cups rained down, shoes and boots pounded against the stands, the band played wild, and the cheerleaders flipped end over end down the sideline. And best of all—better even than the news Coach Huff told me about OU—this time my mom was up in the stands, along with Tommy Don.

And the icing on the cake—Sara was up there too.

She had her a seat right on the fifty-yard line where I could look up and see her grinning any time I wanted. The way I figured it, win or lose, this right here was how football was supposed to be.

"Hey," I yelled as Blaine started onto the field with the rest of the offense. "Have you some damn fun out there for a change, son!"

Blaine wasn't looking to have no fun, though, I don't guess. He hated them Okalah boys down to the last player, but he didn't hate no one as bad as number fifty-five, Covey Wallace, the outside linebacker. Covey was the big blond meaty kid he punched that night out at Wild West Days, and the two of them had been tangling it up since the first play our offense run and it was only getting worse now.

There wasn't but a couple minutes left in the first half, and we got us some decent field position on the forty-five-yard line after Okalah muffed their punt. Our first play was a screen pass into the flats to Blaine. The timing was perfect. He caught it at a full run and made it around right end untouched. Last year, he would've ripped it for a long gainer, maybe even a touchdown, but not now. Covey Wallace tracked him down before he gained ten yards and laid him out flat. That wasn't all, though. He took his sweet time getting up off of Blaine, and before Blaine could pull hisself off the ground, damn old Covey tromped down on his knee—the bad one—on purpose. Man alive, it hurt me to watch it, and there wasn't no doubt Blaine would be out for revenge after that.

Back in the huddle, he took to jawboning Darnell so fierce you could practically see the spit fly. Sure thing he wanted the ball again, but it was too late. Coach done called for a pass to Jake. Blaine's job was to play decoy receiver, but there wasn't no way he'd settle for that right now. Instead, he charged straight into Covey Wallace, and this time Blaine was on top when the whistle blew the incomplete pass dead. He took advantage of it too, grinding his knee so deep in Covey's stomach it's a wonder that Okalah boy didn't break in half.

Dirty gets dirty back. That was Blaine's motto from the get-go.

Didn't help the score none, though. Darnell got bottled up for a loss on the next play, and we was back in punt formation our own selves.

Halftime score: 0 to 0.

While we was in the locker room waiting for Coach to come in and give his speech, Blaine couldn't talk about nothing but Covey Wallace.

"You know what that fool said to me out there?" He slapped a backhand across my chest like it was me he was mad at. "He said, 'How's it feel, Keller? You ain't so tough when you can't get a sucker punch in first.' *Sucker punch!* I'll tell you what, that wasn't no sucker punch I laid on him. I hit him straight-on in the mouth with him looking right at me. It's not my fault he don't know how to duck."

He was more than just a little worked up. I had to tell him, "Look, don't let that kid get to you. We ain't just playing one guy out there. We're playing a whole team."

"Yeah, well," he said. "You bite the head off a snake and the snake'll die."

I didn't know what to say to something like that. Didn't matter anyways. Coach marched in about that time, and I don't believe I ever seen him look so grim. He didn't even face the team but stood over by the row of lockers with his back turned. Even the back of his neck looked mad! For a long time, he kept real still, not saying a word, like he was studying something on the metal locker in front of him, something serious, like an epitaph.

Then finally, without turning around, he started summing up the first half in a real soft voice. I swear, it was scarier than any yelling he could've done. The way he told it, you wouldn't have thought a solitary soul did a lick of good out there, but he gave it to the offense worst of all.

"It looks like the newspapers are right," he said, not a drop of emotion in his voice. He could just as well have been talking about the weather. "We might have a halfway decent team if we had any offense at all. But truth is, we don't, not tonight. I wonder if that's gonna be the story in the paper again tomorrow. I wonder. Is that gonna be what this whole town's talking about for the rest of the year?"

Then a little steam started to build up in his voice. "What am I saying? That's what people's gonna be talking about for a lot longer than a year. They'll be hashing it over till a good hard rain comes and washes the whole town clean out of these hills. 'Cause you don't get chances like this but once every thirty years. Five undefeated seasons in a row. That's what it's all about right here and right now. I wonder, are we gonna blow that chance?"

There's where he usually would've gone into the old call-and-response routine, tossing out lines like a Baptist preacher and waiting for the congregation to throw the answers back. Building it up more and more, making us repeat our answers louder and louder till we're yelling our heads off, chanting, "Fight, Knights, fight!" But he didn't do that. This time, he just turned and walked out the door, leaving us with our mouths hanging open.

Blaine was the first to stand up. "Well, boys, he left it to us. We gotta figure out our own selves whuther we're gonna win this game or not. And there ain't but one way to do it, and that's to bring it to 'em hard and mean. We gotta roll out like thunder and come down like fire."

I always said it. Blaine was a natural-born leader. "Whatta we gonna do, boys?" he yelled.

And we come right back with, "Fight!"

And there it went. We was the congregation again. No doubt about it. We was the congregation, and Blaine was the preacher, sparks in his eyes and his fist pounding the air. Only it wasn't salvation he was hollering about. It was winning. But I guess for Blaine them two things was pretty much the same.

CHAPTER TWENTY-EIGHT

Back out on the field, we took the first kick of the second half, and our boys bucked and elbowed their way clear down to the Okalah twenty-yard line before finally stalling out. On fourth and six, we tried us a field goal, but the ball slammed into the right goalpost and bounced off to the side, no good. Blaine collapsed down on his knees and shook his fists. Just a few feet in front of him—I seen it plain as day—Covey Wallace looked down and blew him a kiss. If Covey hadn't turned around and run off right quick, who knows what Blaine might've done to him.

Through the whole third quarter, the score didn't change. Us defense boys stood our ground and kept Okalah on their own side of the field, and their defense, truth be told, didn't play all that hot, but they didn't need to with our offense misfiring like a forty-year-old pickup truck. At the end of the quarter, Blaine shouldered up to me, his hair sweat-pasted to his forehead, his eyes full to the brim with tired, and said, "What else can I do, Hamp? I'm giving it everything I got, but the team's not there for me. No blocking, bad timing, Coach calling the wrong plays. What do they expect me to do—win the damn game all by myself?"

I just popped him one on the back and told him to hang in there, figuring he must be clean wore out. It wasn't like him to put the blame off on other folks that way.

Finally, a couple minutes into the fourth quarter, our offense got her shifted into gear. Darnell zinged a perfect pass into tight coverage, and Jake scooped the ball up right before it hit the ground. It was about time we went to taking chances, and Darnell pulled it off with an amazing throw. Coach sent in the next play. Do it again.

Just like he was supposed to do, Blaine run out into the flats in case Darnell needed a safety-valve receiver, but it would've been better if he'd stayed in the backfield to block. Two Okalah linemen broke through and chased Darnell out of the pocket. Downfield, Jake was covered just like the play before, but this time Darnell was off balance with four big hairy arms reaching out to wring his neck. He tried to force the pass anyways, but as soon as it left his hand I knew it was a mistake.

The Okalah cornerback intercepted the ball at a full gallop, heading in the opposite direction. The sideline was wide open. There wasn't no one fixing to catch him now, but Blaine tried. I knew the pain in that knee had to be tearing through him from top to bottom, and you could see the hitch in his get-along worse than ever, but that boy had heart.

Then out of nowhere a red and white jersey flashed through the air, a diving block that sliced straight across his thighs, sending him plowing face mask–first into the grass. The Okalah cornerback was already dancing in the end zone when Blaine pulled hisself up and seen what I already knew. Covey Wallace'd cut him down.

Okalah missed their extra point try, but still, that touchdown sucked every ounce of energy there was out of our stadium. Even the electric lights seemed cold. But I didn't give up. Not even near it. If Okalah's second-rate defense could score six points, then ours could score twice that, and I was just the man for the job. All I needed was one good chance.

Okalah wasn't fixing to give me one, though. It was like their coach read my mind. They didn't do nothing but play conservative, running three safe plays and then punting the ball away down the field. They must've figured they'd ruther give the ball up to our offense than let our aces on defense get too close a look at it.

Then, finally, with a little over two minutes left in the game, I got maybe not a good chance, but at least a halfway decent one. Okalah had to punt from deep in their own territory again, and this time their line didn't play it safe enough. The gap couldn't have been more than two feet wide and only opened for a second, but that was enough. I hit it running full speed, but in my mind all the action slowed down: the ball reaching the punter's fingers, the punter's two big steps, his left foot planting in the grass, his right leaving the ground, the black shoe pumping into the brown leather of the ball.

Too late. I'd done blasted off already, flying over one blocker and then the one behind him, my arms stretched out full length, my eyes trained on nothing but that ball. It hadn't no sooner left the punter's foot than I smacked it down with my forearm and sent it whirligigging off across the field. Jerseys—red and white and black and gold—flashed towards it in a blur. Whistles blew like crazy. When the officials finally got that churning dog pile pulled apart, my heart just about jumped out of my chest. There he was, smiling like it was his birthday, little old Tommy Nguyen with the ball wrapped up in his arms.

Kennisaw's ball on the Okalah fifteen-yard line.

It was like someone turned the electricity back on in our fans. The chant started up again, "Hampton! Hampton! Hampton!" I went over and put my arm around Tommy's shoulder to let that crowd know they needed to spread the love around some more, and sure enough they done it.

"Tommy! Tommy! Tommy!"

You better believe, running off the field, I was pumped up higher than a hot-air balloon. Crossing paths with Blaine, I grabbed ahold of his jersey. "Fifteen yards," I hollered. "Just fifteen yards and an extra point, and we got this sucker wrapped up in Christmas paper."

"Don't worry, son," he hollered back. "I got that fifteen yards in my hip pocket."

But just for a second, a shadow flitted over his eyes, and I wondered if he done flashed on the same memory as me. The time, not too long ago, when he said the same thing about Rachel Calloway.

All his years of playing football, Blaine wanted to be the one with the chance for glory. If a first down needed to be made, if a pass needed to be caught, if the team had to have one more score, you can bet Blaine wanted the job. But a feeling in my gut told me right now, with the pressure hanging over the stadium like a big black thunderhead, he was wishing Tommy Nguyen'd recovered that fumble in the end zone instead of on the fifteen-yard line.

First play was a quarterback draw with Darnell following Blaine up the middle for four yards. Then Blaine took it off-tackle, gaining three more. Third and three. Darnell took a keeper into the middle again, but this time the Okalah line held tougher than a barbwire fence, and he didn't get as much as an inch. Fourth down.

Blaine got the call.

The thought crossed my mind that I should ask Coach to put me in as a blocker like Sawyer done with big bad James Thunderhorse, but I decided against it. Last thing Blaine wanted, besides losing the game, was to score a touchdown right now and still have the crowd go to chanting my name.

The play clock ticked down as Darnell stretched out his count, trying to draw Okalah offsides. When that didn't work, he gave it one more hut, and Sweetpea snapped the ball back. Blaine ripped forward, grabbed the handoff, and smashed into the line, head down low and knees pumping up high. Just like the old Blaine. Then for a second, his legs went traitor on him, and he stumbled, almost went down, but somehow found his balance and plunged on ahead, twisting and grinding, taking a hit from first one side and then the other, Okalah hands punching and poking and grabbing from every direction, before he finally crashed to the ground. A four-yard gain.

First down.

He done it, I thought. Wasn't no one going to keep us out of the end zone from this close now. But you know what they say. It ain't over till it's over.

Half the Okalah team must've been on top of Blaine, and

they wasn't in no hurry to get off. Finally, looking kind of woozy, he set up and shook his head back and forth like he needed to rattle his brain back into socket. In front of him, an Okalah player reached down a hand to help him up, and right then's when the bad feeling hit me.

Don't take that hand, I thought. *Don't take it.*

But he did, and next thing you knew, he was standing face to face with Covey Wallace.

Now, from where I was, I couldn't see everything, but I'll take Blaine's word for it. Covey grinned a big ugly grin, leaned in, stared Blaine in the eye, and puckered his lips together. But he didn't blow no kisses this time. This time he spit a big juicy gob smack in Blaine's eye.

Blaine went off like a bottle rocket. Slammed his fist into the side of Wallace's helmet and kept on swinging—crazy roundhouse punches, first into one side of that red helmet, then the other, into the face mask, shoulder pads, anywheres he could make solid contact. Whistles blew right and left. Officials scurried up in a panic and pulled Blaine away. Yellow flags dove to the ground. The whole stadium froze solid.

Darnell and Jake run up from behind and hustled Blaine off down the field while the officials rounded up the Okalah captain for a conference. There wasn't no doubt what the outcome was fixing to be, though. Unsportsmanlike conduct. Fifteen-yard penalty. One minute and twenty-seven seconds left in the game and the end zone as far away as a cold Martian moon.

CHAPTER TWENTY-NINE

After the stadium lights shut down and every last car and truck abandoned the parking lot, Blaine and me walked up into the empty stands. The place looked small and hollow now with the fans gone and nothing but the stars and a few stray streetlight beams to light it. Blaine went up ahead, kicking aside paper cups and popcorn boxes, making his way to the very top row, where he set down even with the fifty-yard line. We'd already showered and changed into our Friday-night clothes, our "Mo" Bettas and Wranglers, boots and black letter jackets. Didn't matter what we wore, though. There wasn't going to be no victory parties tonight.

Slow and easy, I hiked up to the top row too. I had me a sharp pain in the hip, so it hurt to climb them steps like that, but at the top, I stood and looked over the concrete wall at the town out there. Course, it was too dark to make out the actual buildings, but I could see the lights sprinkled down the hillside and into the valley, and I knew by heart what they all belonged to. Decker's Hardware and the bank, the old brick drugstore, Sweet's Café, and, at the far edge, Coleman's Barbeque Hut. Places I'd been to a thousand times.

Then, to the north, climbing up Ninth Street Hill, the lights of the nicer houses shined through the trees, the houses with the wide front porches where girls like Rachel Calloway and Misty Koonce lived. Way across town from me and my mom's place and higher up the hill than Sara's. That was okay, though, I thought, picking out the spot where Sara's house was hid in the dark. There wasn't anything that special higher up on that hill anyways.

"We had that game won." Blaine was setting there staring at the scoreboard like maybe, if he just concentrated hard enough, he could still change the outcome. "We had it won every which way but on the damn scoreboard."

I looked up at the scoreboard too, but I couldn't make it change neither.

"Covey Wallace," Blaine said. "I vote we go find that sonofabitch. He needs his butt kicked. Hard."

"He's all the way back to Okalah by now," I said. "They're probably out partying like it's the end of World War Four, and they're the only ones left on Earth." I didn't care a day-old donut about getting back at anyone. The game was over. We lost. Scrounging around for some scrap of revenge wasn't going to change the score. Far as that went, I figured we'd be better off taking us a cruise out in the country, out to the dirt roads where the woods could swallow you up for a while, and you could feel like part of something a whole lot bigger than winning or losing.

"The play was dead, and he spits in my face," Blaine went on. "Stands right there toe to toe with me, puckers them big fat lips together, and spits in my eye. What am I supposed to do, dance with the fool?"

"He was baiting you," I said. "It's an old trick. They'll call a fifteen-yarder on you and toss you out of the game every time if you out and out bust a guy in the head." I tried not to sound accusing about it, but I don't guess it worked.

"So, what the hell?" Blaine stood up, his face red as a chili pepper. "Is it my fault we lost the game? Is that what you're saying? 'Cause I'll tell you what, I wasn't the one that threw that interception they scored on. I wouldn't have never threw that ball if it was me."

Not wanting to provoke him no more, I didn't answer right off. That stadium never seemed so dead-hollow quiet as it did right then. I shifted from foot to foot trying to think of some way to fill up that hollow feeling, but as usual I couldn't come up with nothing. Blaine was the talker, always had been. He won the argument every time, piled up words like truckloads of bricks, making walls out of them I couldn't break through with a sledgehammer. Sometimes I wondered if he even cared whuther them words was true or if he just wanted to come out on top.

"Let me ask you this." He broke the silence first. "What do you think this is gonna do to Darnell? He's the one has to live with that interception. He'll have to read about it in the paper tomorrow and all week and every year after this when the Okalah game comes back around. He's gonna have to hear about it up and down the halls Monday and every day for the rest of the school year. He'll walk down the street and kids are gonna look at him and say, 'There goes the guy that lost us the Okalah game and threw our five undefeated seasons out with the rest of the garbage.'"

"It wasn't just him on the field," I said. "We was all out there tonight."

Blaine shoved his hands in his letter-jacket pockets. "But that ain't what folks are gonna remember. They're gonna be looking for a scapegoat. That's how people are. And what do you think his girlfriend's gonna do? She won't want to have to mess with him now. No way. Her and nobody else's gonna want to have anything to do with the town goat."

"Cinda's not like that," I said. Cinda was Darnell's girlfriend, had been since sixth grade. "I don't think she even cares if he's on the football team."

"Well, you're a whole lot dumber than you look, then. You think girls around here don't care about that? These girls living up in their big old houses, driving around their brand-new SUVs all over town, they want 'em a football player to show off."

I glanced off at the lights on the hillside. "I think you're selling the girls around here pretty dadgone short."

Blaine didn't even hear that, though. "Wouldn't surprise me none," he said, "if Darnell's dad didn't blow his stack too. Next thing you know, he'll be kicked right out of the family."

I had to give Blaine a close-up look on that one. All the sudden, I understood. He wasn't really talking about Darnell. Not at all. He was talking about hisself. He was afraid of folks calling *him* the goat. Whispering about him behind their hands every time he walked down the street. The topic of sports columns and town gossip and the butt of jokes down at the Rusty Nail. The guy whose girlfriend wouldn't never care for him again and whose dad would kick him flat out of the family like what happened to his brother, Billy.

"Sounds to me like you're making too big a deal out of it," I said. "I mean, listen, we still got the second-best record any team in our division ever had in the whole history of Oklahoma football. Think of it that way."

I guess I should've known Blaine wasn't never going to think of it that way, though.

"Hold on," he said, grabbing my arm. His eyes went all wide like he'd just had him some kind of amazing Bible-style revelation. "I got it. The perfect damn idea. Here's what we'll do, we'll head over to Okalah and find Covey Wallace."

"I don't know—" I started, but I couldn't get nothing in.

"Wait. Just hear me out." He looked away at the football field, like he could see the whole thing unfolding down there. "We find Covey Wallace, and I challenge him to one play. One more down, only with no cheating this time. Just me and him. Fifth and ten, we'll call it. If I make it by him for a score, I get his letter jacket and fly it from the flagpole in front of school all weekend. If I don't make it, then he gets mine."

"Your letter jacket?" I couldn't hardly see Blaine letting loose of his letter jacket for even five minutes, let alone a whole weekend.

"Hey, son, if I can't make ten yards against that fool, then I don't want my letter jacket no more." He was pumped again, his shoulders thrown back and all the slouch gone out of him. I could see something else too, though, just barely, but there it was, a kind of pleading look way down in the shadows of his eyes.

I had to give in then. It was too hard to see Blaine that way. "That's all we'll do, though, right? Just challenge him to one more play. Fifth down and ten."

"That's all. Trust me." He was already charging off, taking them stadium steps two at a time.

CHAPTER THIRTY

It was only a twenty-minute drive to Okalah, but Blaine must've downed three beers on the way, easy. They didn't seem to quench nothing, though. "I don't know what the big deal with college is supposed to be anyways," he said, staring down the headlight beams on the road in front of us. "I mean, how many college teams have gone undefeated as long as we done? That's what I want to know."

"So what are you saying?" I asked. "You're not going to college now at all?" I didn't like the sound of that. I still hoped Blaine would find a way to go to OU even if it wasn't to play football. Them college campuses was awful big places to head off to by yourself.

He wasn't in the question-answering mood tonight, though. "You know how many pro teams have went undefeated as long as we did? None. Only one pro team went *one* season undefeated. So you can just keep the pros too. That's what I'm saying."

"You can go to college for more things than just football," I said, but I didn't make no more headway with that one than the last one.

"No, thank you," he said. "I don't need college, and I don't need the pros. All that's just a step down, as far as I'm concerned. I'm a Knight. That's what I am. That's what I'm always gonna be."

"That don't mean you have to forget—"

Before I could finish, without warning one, he tromped on the brake and swerved off to the shoulder of the road right on the outskirts of Okalah.

"What the hell are you doing?" I hollered. "You just about drove us off in the bar ditch."

"I got something to take care of," he said, tossing a beer can into the backseat. He got out and walked around to the rear end of the Blazer, where he pulled out his old single-shot .410 and a box of shells. He always kept that little old shotgun back there. Just in case, he told people. But it wasn't nothing more than a kid's gun, really, the first one he ever owned, and he only used it to take potshots at jackrabbits in the fields along the back roads outside Kennisaw. Said it was more of a challenge with the single-shot. It was like life, he said. You only got one shot at that too.

But there wasn't no jackrabbits around here, only the Okalah town-limits sign. HOME OF THE OKALAH OUTLAWS, it said in red lettering. POP. 8,953.

He opened the box of shells and slid one into the chamber, and then, before I had a chance to get the window rolled down to say something, he raised the barrel up and squeezed the trigger. *Boom!* That old town-limits sign rocked back and forth, the middle of the thing peppered through with buckshot holes.

For a second there, he smiled a little smile to hisself, but it didn't last long, and that black look settled over him again. He broke the shotgun open, popped out the spent shell, and slid him a fresh one into the chamber.

I had the window rolled down now. "Hey, cut it out! You don't think folks is gonna know who did that after we roll into town?"

Blaine stared at the sign a moment longer. "Yeah," he said, starting back for the driver's side. "We can always hit it again on the way back if we want." He climbed in and set the gun down on the floorboard behind the seat.

"Why don't you put that thing back in the back again," I told him.

"Never know when you'll need you some insurance," he said, and then, there we was, heading off for the lights of town.

Now, the first thing you do when you pull into any small town is cruise up and down Main Street to get the overall feel of the place, and then the next thing you do, if you're a teenager, anyways, is head over to Sonic or whatever kind of burger joint they got, and see if there's any action around.

"This town's dead," Blaine said. "Check it out. There ain't even hardly nobody up at the Sonic."

"Maybe they're already in bed," I said.

"On a Friday night after a football game? Even this town ain't that lame."

As we circled through the Sonic parking lot, he rolled

down the window and yelled at the carhop, asking her where everybody was, trying to sound all innocent, like he wasn't up to nothing but just scouting around for some friends. She was roller-skating her tray full of Cokes along to a car down the way and didn't slow up a notch. "Big party at the armory," she called out over her shoulder.

Blaine turned back to me. "The armory. You know where that is?"

"No clue. It's getting late anyways. Party's probably about over."

"Are you kidding? They ain't gonna end that party till Monday morning."

"Well, I sure don't know where to find it."

"That's okay. I mean, how hard could an armory be to find in a Podunk town like this?"

He was right on that one. It wasn't but just a few minutes before we come across a good-size line of cars parked along the side of the road over on the west side of town, and sure enough, we followed them right up to the parking lot, where there wasn't space one left open. The armory itself was this gigantic building made out of good old red Oklahoma stone with the 45th Division Thunderbird emblem fixed on the front wall. Over on the lawn, they had them an old green World War II cannon, and next to that a pack of high school kids in red jackets was hanging around, talking and laughing. There was another group congregated up under the big arched doorway of the building, and here and there you could see a couple walking together or a stray single kid heading across the lawn with his hands in his pockets.

"I guess this is where everyone is," I said as we cruised real slow through the full parking lot.

"Yep," Blaine said. "This place is so packed they must be celebrating Asshole Day or something. I know they can't be having a victory dance. Even Okalah fools ain't stupid enough to think they won fair and square. I'll tell you what, if that Covey character's around here, I'm gonna have to just lay him right out on the spot. One punch and down, just like last time."

"Hey now," I said. "Remember what your dad told you about how much trouble you could get in trying something like that in any town other than Kennisaw. Besides, I thought we done agreed you wasn't gonna do nothing but challenge him to a fifth and ten for letter jackets."

Blaine screwed his face up like he was having to step over a cow pie. "Who are you, his mother or something?"

"Before we come over here, you said—"

"Okay, okay, don't get all sensitive on me. Damn." He turned back to the windshield. "Well, well, what do we have here?" Ahead, a row of real pretty girls set side by side up on the stone wall that run along the side of the parking lot. Every one of them wore red Okalah jackets. "I bet one of them nasty little things could tell us where old Covey is."

He pulled up in front of the wall where the girls set and rolled down the window. "Hey, can any of you pretty ladies tell me where my good friend Covey Wallace is at?"

A cute brunette hopped down off the wall. "Who wants to know?"

"Just a couple big shots with the circus is all." There he went, pulling another one of his wild stories out of nowhere.

"Shoot," the brunette said. "You guys ain't with no circus."

"Sure we are. We done traveled the whole entire country back and forth two dozen times. Dallas, Baton Rouge,

212

St. Louis. You name it. Lion taming's what I do. It's pretty dangerous. Chairs and whips and all like that. A guy gets used to it, though."

The girl looked around him in towards me. "Who's your friend there, the giant?"

"No way," Blaine said. "The giant's ten foot tall. His head alone's the size of a beer barrel. This here's the strong man. Name's Mamboosala."

"Really?" She fixed her eyes right on mine now. "How much can you lift?"

"Oh, he don't talk," Blaine cut in. "Never could. Born that way. But he's strong, all right. You should see his act. He wears him this wild leopard-skin-type deal and big black fur boots. Throws barbells up in the air with weights on 'em the size of snow tires. The crowd goes crazy. They're throwing popcorn, yelling his name—Mamboosala, Mamboosala, Mamboosala. Just like that."

"He sure looks strong." She smiled at me. Usually, I wouldn't have thought a cute girl like her would have no more interest in me than she would in reading *Moby Dick* on a Saturday night, but she sure seemed to have something more in that smile of hers than just plain old nice.

Blaine gave me a glance, then turned back to her. "Yep, he's strong, all right, but the problem is he never was too bright."

"Hey now," I said. "I make better grades than you."

"Did you hear that?" He slapped me one on the shoulder. "The first words he ever spoke. It's a miracle."

She stepped back and crossed her arms. "You're full of it. You guys ain't even old enough to be in any circus. What's them jackets you got on anyways?" She squinted at the K on the front of Blaine's jacket. "Wait a minute, y'all's from Kennisaw." She turned around to her friends. "Hey, these boys are from Kennisaw."

"Well," said the little redhead from her perch up on the wall. "We kicked your butts tonight, didn't we?" Her friends had a good laugh over that one.

Blaine's jaws tightened on him, and that vein around his temple pumped a couple times, but he kept hisself from blowing up.

"What do y'all want with Covey?" the brunette asked.

Blaine forced a smile back on his face. "We just want to challenge him to a little rematch," he said. "We got us a bad call by the officials out there, and we figure it'd only be fair to line it up again and see who really won."

"Bad call, huh?" the brunette said. "I'll bet."

The redhead hopped down from the wall and waltzed over next to her friend. "Y'all looking for Covey Wallace? I know where he is."

The brunette one punched her arm. "Shawna, don't you dare tell them where he is."

"Why not? If he wants to drag some little blond tramp from another school over here, then he can sure talk to these guys too."

"All's we want to do is discuss that rematch." Blaine looked at me. "Ain't that right, Mamboosala?"

I didn't say anything. Truth be told, I wasn't real hot on that Mamboosala stuff.

Little old Shawna walked up closer to the window and eyed us over. A strand of her red hair come loose across the side of her face, and she pulled it back. "There's a big beer bust going on at the pavilion out by the lake. He's out there. You know where the lake is?"

"Yeah, we know where it is."

"Well, he's got a big white pickup with an eagle decal spread out on the back window. And if he ain't at the pavilion, check the little dirt road that runs alongside the lake out there. That's where he likes to go parking."

"Shawna!" the brunette said, her eyes flared up wide. "How do you know that's where he likes to go parking?"

Shawna didn't answer that. She just stared in at Blaine and said, "And I want you to do me a favor too. You tell him it was me that told you where he was."

"Sure thing," he said. He started to roll the window up but stopped for a second. "You know what? You all oughta hang around. Who knows, we might stop back by when we get done and show you Okalah girls what a real football player is." He gave a wink, rolled the window on up, and pulled off.

"I don't want to stop back by here," I told him.

"Why not? Them girls ain't half bad."

"I just don't want to, that's all."

"Hey," he said, opening hisself up another beer. "You back me up with what I gotta do with Covey, and we'll go wherever you want to after that."

CHAPTER THIRTY-ONE

It was almost midnight by the time we got out to the lake. I was thinking about me and Sara's early-morning walk in the country, counting down the hours of sleep I could still get, when the little pavilion come into view, snuggled back in the scrub oaks on the left side of the road. Between a couple posts, someone had strung up a homemade paper sign with the score of the game scrawled across it in red spray paint, and next to that, they had them a pitiful-looking cartoon of a knight hanging from a stick-figure gallows pole.

"What do you think they'd do if I put a shotgun blast through that little sign of theirs?" Blaine asked.

"Probably run and tell the police."

"Let 'em."

Citronella eased down the bumpy road, and next thing

you know, we seen a little bonfire flaring up in among the twisted trees. You could hear a whoop and a fit of laughing coming from off that way, but you couldn't see nothing more than the black silhouettes of the kids moving around in front of the flames. Truck after truck was parked along the roadside, but not a one of them had an eagle decal stretched out across the back window.

"I got a bad feeling about this," I said. "I think we oughta just head on back home."

"You need to get off that kick about going home," Blaine said. "We can't go back now."

"Why not?"

"We just can't."

We kept on bouncing down the dirt road, the moon shining on Citronella's hood, black shadows of tree limbs making patterns in the pale light. The sounds of the party faded off behind us, and finally we come to the dirt road that circled the lake.

"This must be the road that girl was talking about," Blaine said, easing to a stop. "Wait here. I'll take a little reconnaissance run up ahead to see if she was telling the truth about our buddy Covey going parking down there."

He climbed out and, real quiet, snuck down the road and around the turn. Soon as he was out of sight, first thing I done was I reached behind the seat, pulled up his .410, and slid that smooth little red shell out of the chamber and stuffed it in my jacket pocket. The way I figured it, no one was going to kill any more signs tonight. Or anything else.

I rolled down the window and took a deep breath. This wasn't where I wanted to be. Not one bit. My life had been changing the last few weeks, opening up in front of me like it never done before. The way I thought, the ideas that run through my mind when I was by myself, was starting to make more sense. The reason how come wasn't clear to me yet, but I felt like I'd started down a new road somehow. But now here I was on the outskirts of a foreign town, staring through Citronella's cracked windshield. The day I had planned with Sara was a long ways away, and this dark road that Blaine led us down wasn't the one I wanted to be on.

Only a couple minutes went by before he come creeping back into view. I tried to think of one more argument for turning around and heading home, but I knew my real best chance was if he didn't find no trace of Covey Wallace. The hope for that pretty much dried up, though, as soon as Blaine opened the door and gave me the biggest mean grin I'd seen on him yet.

"We got our man," he said. "Come on, let's go."

I stared out the front window. "I been doing some thinking. Why don't we just leave it alone. I mean, we got beat. So what? It's not the end of the world."

"Maybe not for you." Blaine looked away, then back. "But forget it. You stay here. I'll do it by myself. And when we get back home, I'll just tell folks you couldn't be bothered with sticking up for the honor of the team. You just said, 'Forget the Kennisaw Knights. They don't mean nothing to me.' That's what I'll tell 'em."

"You know that ain't true."

Blaine reached in and pulled the driver's seat forward. "Yep, I'll tell everyone now that you're a cinch to get you some big OU scholarship and everything, you couldn't care less about the old Kennisaw gang. Forget your old friends. You got bigger plans." He pulled the .410 from behind the seat and cradled it in his arm.

"What are you getting that thing out for?" I asked him.

"If you ain't gonna back me up, I'm gonna take some backup of my own."

I didn't like the sound of that. "Look," I said, "I didn't say I wouldn't go with you. I just don't think this is the way to handle it."

Blaine looked down towards the lake. "I ain't asking you for a vote. You can come or not. That's up to you." He shut the door.

"Aw hell," I said to myself, and opened my door up.

"Attaboy, Mamboosala," he said, shooting a grin my way. "Welcome back to the team."

"Don't call me Mamboosala," I told him.

At the crossroads, we turned south. Off to the left, the lake stretched out smooth and silvery black under the bright moon, and on the far shoreline, trees rose up like dark clouds of smoke. The rank old smell of dead fish wafted up from the bank. Behind us the road run long and straight, but the way we was headed was crooked, a sharp curve hiding what was to come.

So far, there wasn't no sign of Covey's truck, but when we rounded the curve, I seen it, first just the tail end jutting out from behind the brush, and then as we drew up closer, the wings of that eagle decal spreading wide across the back window. My stomach felt about like it dropped through a dark dungeon trapdoor when I seen that.

"There's our boy," Blaine said. "Keep low and close to the side of the road and don't make no noise." He sounded just like he did when we played army games as kids and he was the sergeant telling me what to do.

Real slow, we moved on up towards the pickup till, some thirty yards away, I heard someone whistling a country tune.

There he was on the far side of the pickup. His back was turned but his thick neck and blond crew cut gave him away. A few yards closer, you could hear the trickle of water against the ground.

"He's taking a piss," Blaine whispered. "This is perfect. Watch me put the fear of God into this fool."

Holding the shotgun with the barrel pointed down towards the road, Blaine circled the truck, waving for me to come up on the other side. Covey's shoulders shrugged as he hitched up his pants.

"Surprise!" Blaine shouted, swinging up the barrel of the gun.

"What the hell?" Covey staggered back a couple steps. His letter jacket was unbuttoned down the front, and he wasn't wearing no shirt underneath.

"It's judgment day," Blaine said. "Now step away from the truck over there. Hamp, come on around here and help me watch our good buddy here."

I walked around the truck, but if Blaine wanted me to look like some kind of tough henchman thug, then he was in for a disappointment.

"What's going on out there?" a voice called from inside the truck. It sounded familiar.

"Tell your girlfriend to come on out," Blaine ordered.

"No way," Covey said. He started forward, but Blaine jabbed the gun barrel his way, and he stopped short.

"Hey, you in there," Blaine called over his shoulder. "Come on out here. We got something for you."

"Okay," the girl's voice said. "Hold your horses."

The driver's side door was already open, and it jostled a little as the girl slid out.

Blaine laughed. "I should've known. Misty damn Koonce. Live and in person."

"Blaine, you idiot," she said. "What are you doing here?" She wore a white sweater and her Rockies blue jeans and she was barefoot. Her blond hair was messed up on one side, but she still looked real pretty in the moonlight.

Right away, I wanted to tell her it was all just a joke to keep her from getting scared, but at the same time, I was mad at her for being here with Covey. Ain't that the craziest thing? There shouldn't have been reason one for it to matter one way or the other to me, but when it come to girls, there's been more times than I can count when my feelings didn't make a lick of sense.

"Your sweater's inside out," Blaine told her.

"No, it's not," she said, checking it anyways.

"Made you look." Blaine's voice had more sour in it than fun, though.

Covey stepped over and put his arm around her. "Look," he said. "You guys lost the game. Why don't you just take it like a couple of men?"

That called Misty's attention over my way for the first time. She shook her head. "I wouldn't have expected something like this out of you, Hampton Green, but I guess wherever Blaine goes, you gotta go too."

I shoved my hands in my jacket pockets and looked away.

"Hamp don't care what you think about him," Blaine said, stepping over as casual as you please towards Covey. He was holding the shotgun crossways close to his chest now. "We're only out here for one reason, and you know what it is."

" 'Cause you're losers?" Covey didn't step back an inch this time.

"The boy's a smartass." Blaine glanced my way, then looked along the barrel of the .410, pretending to wipe something off the sight.

"Hey, y'all," Misty said. "I'm hungry. You got any money? I could sure use some pizza. I don't have my purse on me, and Covey spent all his money on his stupid beer."

"We're not out here to give you charity," Blaine told her.

"All the pizza places are closed by now," I put in, trying to sound sympathetic about it.

"Well," she said, tilting her head sideways in that cute way she had, "maybe they got some weenies left up at the bonfire. I like them weenies when they're good and crispy. You know, kinda black and split down the middle. I'd eat 'em straight off the stick that way. Maybe dunk 'em in ketchup first if they got any."

"Shut the hell up!" Blaine waved the gun barrel in her direction, not so much threatening as just for emphasis. "In case you ain't noticed, we got some serious business to transact here."

"God." Misty rolled her eyes. "What's got you in such a bad mood?"

Covey squeezed her shoulder. "I'll tell you why they're in a bad mood. They got a bug up their ass 'cause they're fixing to go down in history as the team that blew the big five-undefeated-season record. Ain't that right, Keller?"

Blaine pointed the .410 square at Covey's white stomach now. And this time there wasn't no doubt he meant it for a threat. "You know what you pulled there at the end, Wallace. You know it and I know it. Why don't you tell her?"

Old Covey just gave him a smirk back, though. "I ain't telling nobody nothing. Now you better put that little six-year-old's gun up before you get yourself in some real trouble 'cause—I'll tell you what—my cousin's on the police force here, and they don't put up with idiots coming in from Kennisaw waving guns around."

"Well," Blaine said, "if you ain't gonna tell it, then I sure don't mind telling it myself. Your boyfriend here spit in my face after I made us a first down out there tonight." He aimed the words at Misty, but it sounded like he could've been talking to the whole town of Kennisaw. "That's how come I hit him. If anyone'd seen what really happened, they never would've called a penalty on me or kicked me out of the game, and I'd be at my own hometown party right now."

"Tell him about playing the down over," I said. "Tell him about fifth and ten for letter jackets. That's all we come out here for."

Blaine shook his head. "I think it's a little late for fifth and ten."

"What's fifth and ten?" Misty said. I swear, that girl could sound chipper in the middle of a hurricane.

"Don't pay no attention to 'em," Covey told her. "They ain't gonna do nothing. Keller ain't got the balls or he wouldn't be out here with a little old .410 popgun."

"You just said the wrong thing." Blaine's voice was so cold now it even gave me the chills. "You're gonna be the one with no balls if you don't own up to what you done and apologize." He lowered the gun barrel so's it pointed just below Covey's silver belt buckle.

Covey stood his ground, though. "Hell, I ain't apologizing to no one, especially not you."

"You got ten seconds. Just apologize and say you really lost the game. That's all."

"Blaine," I said, stepping up next to him. "Come on, son."

Misty leaned in close to Covey's side. "I don't like this." All the shine was wore off her voice now. "This ain't funny anymore."

"Sure it is," Covey told her. "Everything Keller does is funny 'cause he's the joke of the whole county. That's all he's gonna be from here on out."

"Hey," I said. "You don't got no right talking like that." I glanced at Blaine, but he only stared straight on ahead.

The barrel of the .410 stuck out just a few yards from Covey, smooth and blue-black without a pinch of sparkle anywheres on it.

"Apologize," Blaine said through gritted teeth.

Covey just threw him another lopsided smirk. "Forget it."

"Apologize."

I was busy squeezing the shell I took out of that .410 so hard it's a wonder it didn't explode in my pocket. Still, staring down at his hand against the dark metal of the gun, I couldn't think nothing but *Don't do it, don't do it, don't squeeze that trigger.*

"Come on, Misty," Covey said, trying to sound bored. "We done wasted too much time on these zeroes already."

"You ain't going nowhere," Blaine said.

"Who's gonna stop me? You sure ain't man enough to do it."

Blaine's finger held taut against the curve of the trigger. There was something strange about it, foreign, like it couldn't really be a part of the same boy I met that Fourth of July at Leonard Biggins Park.

Don't do it, I kept thinking. *Don't do it.* Almost like a prayer.

For a second, his finger relaxed, the coil of it melting away a little, and I thought maybe things would turn back to something more familiar, but they didn't. Instead, that finger curled up again, and there wasn't nothing I could do before it jerked back with one quick snap. The hammer kicked against the firing pin, and a hollow metal *clack* echoed out across the lake.

And time stopped.

It was Misty froze there in her bare feet, the moonlight silvery on her hair, and Covey next to her, his red letter jacket hanging open, his white stomach pooching through, his fists clenched, and his chin poked out. It was Blaine gripping that old shotgun he'd slipped a shell into less than an hour ago. Our whole past was there too—the past that was and the pasts that could've been—and the futures that might come. And I seen how I needed to be there. Right in that moment, I was the best friend Blaine ever had, but not for the reasons either one of us believed in coming out to this place.

"Ha!" Covey laughed. "I knew that thing wasn't loaded."

Blaine stared down at the gun like it played him a dirty trick.

"I swear," Covey went on. "If it wasn't two of you fools here, I'd beat you silly, Keller."

"Shut up!" Blaine hollered. "I'm done messing with you." He swung the gun back like a baseball bat, ready to whup it into Covey's big white face, but I already predicted it and caught ahold of the barrel and ripped the thing out of his hands before he could start it back around.

"What the hell are you doing?" he screamed at me, red-faced and near to bawling.

I looked him in the eye. "It's time to head home."

"You don't tell me when it's time to go home."

"It's over."

"No it ain't." He grabbed at the gun, but I heaved it over his head into the high grass along the lake.

"You're a damn Judas," he said. I never seen him look so mad as right then. "You know that? Judas down to the bone. You might as well do what he done and go hang yourself from one of these trees." He glanced off for a second towards where I thrown his gun, but that was just a decoy before he whipped back around, his fist flying straight for my mouth. I seen that one coming too, though, and blocked it with my left forearm. With my right hand, I grabbed a fistful of his letter jacket and slung him down on the road. He tried to scramble up, but it was too late. I was on his back, pressing his arms hard against the dirt.

"Get off me," he hollered. "Get off me, you backstabbing sonofabitch." He struggled and twisted, but I always was the stronger one.

"Let him up, and I'll take over." Covey was standing right over us. "I owe him one."

"You stay back," I warned him. "You just take Misty and get in your truck and get out of here."

"Let me up!" Blaine sputtered.

Covey looked down at Blaine and then at me, sizing up what he ought to do.

"Come on," Misty told him. "Let's go. You don't want to mess with Hampton."

For a moment longer, he stared down, but he didn't make a move. "I ain't got nothing against you, Hampton. But I don't want to see Keller over here in our town no more. You all got that?"

"Go on and get out of here, right now." I stared him a hard one straight in the eye. "Get in your truck and move on or you're gonna wish you did."

Without trying on a comeback, Covey nodded and backed away. He put his arm around Misty's shoulder, and they headed towards the truck.

Blaine tried bucking me off, but I rode him down. "Let me up!" he bellowed out again. "Can't you see I gotta do this? Don't you get it? I ain't getting no scholarships. I'm gonna be stuck around here with this damn night hanging around my neck for the rest of my life if I don't do something."

I pressed his arms harder into the dirt. "Son, you almost got a lot worse than that hanging around your neck, you know that?"

He didn't answer.

"You know that?" I cranked it up a notch this time.

There was a long pause, and then finally he come out with it, not loud but loud enough.

"Yeah, I know."

I waited till Covey's truck started down the road before I let go of Blaine's arms and got off him. Real slow, he pulled hisself up to his knees but no further than that. Everything around was real still, except the trickle of the leaves on the dirt road and the cold wind swooping across the lake.

Then his shoulders started to heaving. His whole body shook, but he wouldn't raise his head. He couldn't even let his best friend since fourth grade see his tears. I wanted to tell him to forget about that old game. That wasn't all he was. His whole life wasn't made up of pride over something you really wasn't and records that was bound to be broke and legends that was only half true in the first place.

227

Forget all that stuff for a while, I wanted to say. Just look out at the way the lake is, the moon on the ripples, the stars rising up and down on the water, the trees on the far bank over there. That's what there is to be a part of. That's something that lasts.

But I knew it wouldn't help. Blaine couldn't see nothing even close to that right now.

CHAPTER THIRTY-TWO

The sun rose up over the oaks, just a sliver at first, and then finally it hung fat and orange over the treetops. The sky stretched out a deep blue, and there was a little chill in the air. I brung me a blanket along, though, and me and Sara set on the hillside with it draped around our shoulders.

"I'm glad we came out here," she said. "I might not get many more chances. My parents are planning on moving back to Oklahoma City next summer."

"I might not get that many more chances neither," I said. "If things go right between my mom and Tommy Don, she might end up moving off to Santa Fe. And then I'll be in college next fall."

"Me too."

I glanced at her, a real quick one, before turning away. I

still wasn't comfortable with trying to look at her too much all at once, but I figured it wouldn't be long before I would be. And then maybe I could talk to her about what happened with Blaine too. That was something I couldn't tell nobody about yet, but when the time come, it was a sure bet she'd be the first one I'd turn to.

"I don't know if you know it," I started in after a while. "But they got a real good medical school over at the University of Oklahoma."

"I know they do," she said. "That's where I'm going."

I nodded. "Me too. If they offer me a scholarship. Coach seems to think it's pretty sure they will."

I checked her out just long enough to catch her smile.

"I hope they do," she said.

"Football's gonna get me there." I looked back off at the tree line. "But who knows what direction I'll head in after that. I might just go into wildlife management if I can."

I could feel her studying me over for a moment. "You're not saying that because of how the game turned out last night, are you?"

"Naw. It's something I been thinking about for a while now."

"Because even if you all didn't win that game, you were pretty amazing. They couldn't counter your blitz worth anything."

I had to laugh at that. "Since when do you know about countering blitzes?"

She wrapped her arms around her knees and smiled again. "I've been reading up."

"Really?"

"A little."

I don't know which I appreciated more—that she'd been studying up on football or that she never said a thing about what Blaine pulled at the end of the game.

When the sun had climbed a good ways up, I took her on that old path that led through the woods and higher up to one of my favorite places, the rock cliffs that looked out on Lake Hawkshaw. All around the hills was just crackling with yellows and reds and oranges. Ironwood and Spanish oak, dwarf chestnut, Chickasaw plum and mulberry and a bunch of other stuff I'd learned the names of.

"Look over here," I said when we got up top. "You can see where T. Roy Strong and a lot of the other Knights carved their names in the cliff."

T. Roy's name was carved bigger than anyone else's, and further on up the face of the rock, a girl named Wendy had carved her out a mathematical equation that added her name to his and equaled out to LOVE 4-EVER. Fact was, more than one girl put her name up with T. Roy's, but I didn't point that out right then.

Lower down on that same rock, me and Blaine had chiseled our names in with our trusty barlow knives. Even though Blaine's name was a good bit smaller than T. Roy's, it was the deepest one on the whole cliff. Next to it, he carved in his rushing record too, but Anton Mack of Sawyer done broke it already this season by twenty-three yards.

"It's funny," Sara pointed out. "You can tell the older names because they're not as deep as the newer ones. I guess the wind smooths them out a little each year."

"I guess so." I never noticed it before, but she was right as rain.

The best view out of the whole place was at the top of the

231

largest rock, so I took her hand and helped her climb up with me. Over in one direction, you could see Lake Hawkshaw stretching out between a frame of oaks and cottonwoods and rangy old sycamores. The other way, down in the valley, bits and pieces of Kennisaw stuck up through the trees—the courthouse, the bank, the Methodist church, and the lights of the football stadium.

Looking off at that, I had me one of my time-stopping moments. It just come on without me even trying. I seen myself in the future coming back to town, not as a big hero returning to give a speech at Leonard Biggins Park or nothing, but just for old times' sake. There I was, driving down Main Street, Sara riding with me, leaning into my shoulder. The football banners, like always, stretching from light pole to light pole, the store windows colored up with painted-on cheers, and the old men roaming the sidewalks. Only now they was slapping the backs of a new crop of football boys.

And it was funny, but I could picture myself stopped at the light where Main hits Konawah, looking out the side window at a high school kid in his black and gold letter jacket, the new starting tailback. But you know what? It wasn't an old man talking to that boy there. It was Blaine. Blaine wearing him a beat-up fishing cap and a flannel shirt, one hand clapped on the boy's shoulder, the other one stretched out in the air like he was pointing to something real big and far away.

I couldn't see the next part clear, though. The part about whuther I'd pull over and talk to Blaine or whuther me and Sara would just drive off the other direction. I didn't know if there'd be anything left to say.

"You know." Sara's voice brought me back to the hilltop.

"I've heard that when you come home after being away at college, your hometown is supposed to look smaller. Do you think that's true?"

I nodded. "It already does."

I turned back to look at the lake again. It stretched out wide and green, and on the other side, more hills rose up, rolling away one after the other till they disappeared in a gold-brown haze.

"So," Sara said. "You ready to head down and try some of those sandwiches I made?"

"Just a minute," I said. "I want to freeze this picture for just a second more."

The wind was picking up, making choppy little waves in the lake and rattling the leaves in the blackjack trees. That Oklahoma wind blowing like always, year after year, sanding down them rocky cliffs bit by bit. One day, they'd wear smooth and slick as the sixth day of creation, and no one would even be able to tell where the old Knights of the hill country carved their names. And that'd be all right. It was carving them that mattered, not how many people come along to read them.

"Okay," I said. "I'm ready. But how about we take the long way back?"